HOARDING

A collection of short stories
And one play

Pat Mullan

Also by Pat Mullan

NOVELS

The Circle of Sodom
Blood Red Square
Last Days of the Tiger
Creatures of Habit
A Deadly Gamble

POETRY

Childhood Hills
Awakening
Knowing
Legacy
James Dickey's Poetry: The Religious Dimension
Daffodil
Bicycle Ride (in Crannóg magazine)

SHORT STORIES

Galway Girl (in WOW anthology)
Tribunal (in Galway Noir)
The Last Blow (in Noir by Noir West)
Screwed
Endings
The Avenger

ANTHOLOGIES

Galway Noir (Akashic Books & Brandon Books)
Noir by Noir West (Arlen House)
Dublin(City-Pickseries)

Pat Mullan

HOARDING

A collection of short stories
And one play

An ATHRY HOUSE Book

HOARDING
By Pat Mullan

An ATHRY HOUSE book

ISBN-13: 978-0-9838652-6-1
ISBN-10: 0983865264

This book is a work of fiction. Any reference to historical events, real people, or real locales is used fictitiously. Other names, characters, places and incidents are either products of the author's imagination or used fictitiously. Any resemblance to actual events, locales, or persons, living or dead, is entirely coincidental.

Cover design by BEAUTeBOOK

Praise for Pat Mullan

"Pat Mullan is a natural born storyteller with a gripping, engaging style. He may just be the next big thing in Irish crime fiction." **Jason Starr, author of LIGHTS OUT**

"Just when I'd lost faith in thrillers, along comes this humdinger to revive my joy in the art" -- **Ken Bruen, St.Martin's Press author of 'The Guards**

"You know you're reading a good thriller when you start to cast it for the movie before you've even finished." -- **Eithne Hannigan, BOOK REVIEWS, CONNEMARA LIFE magazine**

"An even mix of Crichton and Clancy and written equally as well. It's a classic page-turner and almost comes across as though it had been adapted from a screenplay" -- **Pod-Dy Mouth**

"With rapid-fire pacing and well-drawn characters, Mr. Mullan takes the reader on a magic carpet ride all over the United States, England, Belgium, Switzerland and Hong Kong to weave a tale most evil and scary. Pat Mullan is a mature and knowledgeable writer who puts together a thriller with the best of them. An excellent read!" **Shelley Glodowski, Reviewer, MIDWEST BOOK REVIEW.**

"An entertaining and thrilling read of the first order...the chilling suspense will keep you restless !!!" -- **Narayan Radhakrishnan, New Mystery Reader**

Pat Mullan would like to express his appreciation to the Clifden Arts Week for his long association and for his warm welcome each year from Carmel Hanley and the children of Clifden Community School.

He would especially like to thank Brendan Flynn.

CONTENTS

The Mayo Clinic describes hoarding as 'a *disorder; a persistent difficulty discarding or parting with possessions because of a perceived need to save them'*

Hoarding

The hoarding of sweets during Lent, of money in a sock, of potatoes in a pit, of clothes and shoes, of indulgences against sin, of emotions against hardship

We are downsizing and decluttering. We are re-discovering the hoard in our attic. A hoard acquired over many years. We are faced with a major decision: select only the most important things to keep. But very little of our attic hoard seems unimportant. As we uncover them, or re-discover them, each unlocks past memories: huge boxes of photos that pre-date the digital camera, letters (love letters too), old magazines, books and more books, old suitcases packed with clothing that we will never wear again but retain the sense of smell of a special day, event, or time. Memories! How do we declutter memories? Many memories that have been under lock and key for years, remaining unopened until now. As we unpack our attic we turn the key in those locks and our past is recreated. But we can only unlock it in our imagination. You will see those memories of Sweeney unfold in *Images of Life.*

And we ask: does the past really exist?

Does the past exist, I wonder, or is it a library of videos, some special, some not so special organized to entertain or even to frustrate, filled with laughter or sorrow, or people we loved, disliked, or even hated. Why would we store these images and why do they run without our wish why do they interrupt when we don't want them why can't we retrieve one that we do want do you know what I mean do you have a library of your past do you share a past event are we connected in some way is the past imaginary did it really exist

I thought of all of that as I sat at the breakfast table, leafing through Seamus Heaney's *Wintering Out.* My wife said that we should choose a poem to read at breakfast, to start the day, to contemplate, to soothe the savage soul. And we did.

Galway Kinnell is one of my favourite poets and we share the same love at breakfast: poetry and porridge (which he calls Oatmeal, being an American).

Lost at Breakfast
Oh, how I lose myself

I get trapped by Galway Kinnell
Reading his Oatmeal as I try
To eat my morning porridge
And I forget to put the milk away

Oh, how I lose myself

Our poetry reading at breakfast
Is the food that starts our day
Blended with organic oats
It fuels our body and our mind

Oh, how I lose myself

Kinnell said that oatmeal
Should not be eaten alone
That an imaginary companion is best
So he ate with John Keats and said that
He'd invite Patrick Kavanagh to join him
So I have invited Galway Kinnell to share
His Oatmeal with me today

Oh, how I lose myself

I met Seamus Heaney at St Columb's College where we boarded for four years. That memory makes me feel close to Seamus again as I read *A Northern Hoard* from his *Wintering Out.* The poem's five sequences search Heaney's hoard of emotion about the dark unremitting world of his Northern Irish home-place. He has deserted that world but his poetic soul drags him back, makes him fuse his sense of the present with a hoard of anguish : *The touch of love, Your warmth heaving to the first move, Grows helpless in our old Gomorrah, We petrify or uproot now.*

But I have no words to follow Seamus. It does make me take stock of my own hoarding: books, letters, photographs, clothes, memories, experiences, the flotsam and jetsam of life, and an attic filled with boxes of time capsules. But I don't need to open those time capsules to see what's inside. I've hoarded the best, and the worst, in the deepest vault in my mind. I can see my great-aunt Maggie in her day-long churning of the butter in our farmhouse kitchen. I can feel the motes in my eyes, from saving the peat for our fire. I can still sense the fear I felt as an altar-boy on display facing the congregation at the Sunday mass. And the dread that sank deep inside the day I was abandoned to my boarding life at St Columb's College. I've hoarded it well. It is very durable. But I've hoarded good memories too, especially of the people who have enriched my life.

The Mayo Clinic describes hoarding as 'a *disorder; a persistent difficulty discarding or parting with possessions because of a perceived need to save them. A person with hoarding disorder experiences distress at the thought of getting rid of the items. Excessive accumulation of items, regardless of actual value, occurs'* But they seem to be focused on the most extreme debilitating aspect of hoarding. I never considered my hoarding as a serious impediment to myself or my friends or family. My hoarding started when I was a young boy, accumulating pens and pencils and school leftovers, such as used erasers (or rubbers as we called them).

And stamps ! At first I tore any and every stamp off letters and other mail that arrived at home. Stamp collecting became my great love, my great passion. I compiled a large album of choice stamps from various countries. But my prize was a rare black one penny stamp which I found on a family legal document in our attic. I never asked permission. I gently pried it from the document and gave it star position in my album.

I took that album with me on the day I entered boarding school at St. Columb's, a place of strict discipline and ritual. Every evening we were dispatched to the study hall where we each had our own desk. That's where I kept my album. It was comforting to take it out and imagine that I had gone to one of the exotic countries from my collection. Until the evening I reached in the desk and discovered that my album was gone. I knew that it was stolen. But I was afraid to report it. My heart felt empty at the loss. It almost cured my hoarding. The emotional impact was not worth it. Why hoard material things that are so precious that it's too hurtful to lose them?

It wasn't until I was older that I learned that my penny black was the world's first adhesive postage stamp used in a public postal system. It was first issued in England on 1 May 1840, but was not valid for use until 6 May. The stamp features a profile of Queen Victoria. It is one of the world's most iconic stamps. Because it's the world's first stamp, it's very valuable. Rare penny blacks are valued at tens of thousands of pounds and have increased in price for decades. So that knowledge has made my loss even more painful.

When I lived in London I often went to plays and readings in the Royal Court theatre. One evening I was captured by the performance and intensity of a young Scottish actor, Brian Cox, starring in Ron Hutchinson's *Rat in the Skull*, a play as hard as the 'troubles' in Northern Ireland. On a subsequent evening he sat near me in the audience for an evening of poetry reading by Paul Muldoon, among others. I later joined them in the pub next door. So I have watched Brian as he has climbed higher in his profession in Hollywood. He is currently the Golden Globe-winning star of HBO's hit show *Succession*.

But it is hoarding that has brought him to my attention again. Appearing on BBC Radio recently, Brian revealed that he has more outfits than his wife, the actor Nicole Ansari. "I am a bit of a hoarder. I have a thing about clothes," he tells, "It is one of those things you are left with, an insecurity. It has to come out somewhere." Cox's father died when he was eight years old and his mother suffered with severe mental illness in the following years. The poverty that marked out his life then, the actor admits, has also made him "cautious" with money in adult life: "I can be a bit parsimonious at times."

That's another type of hoarding. The type often learned in the home in Ireland where the necessities of life was not abundant and frugality ruled the day. My mother was an expert at fixing shoes by carving leather out of other shoes, at making jackets out of old Spillars flour bags; conservation of scarce resources which could only be supported by the hoarding of all usable, or reusable materials. And she hoarded money too; the occasional five or ten pound note which she stashed away in a place only known to her and St. Anthony.

But I do not suffer from that kind of hoarding.

Recently I flew from Ireland to New York. As usual I stuffed a paperback - a fat one, about 400 pages - into my carry-on bag. I had really wanted to take a hardback I'd been reading at home but that was impractical. As my fellow travellers and I waited at the boarding gate in Shannon, many of us fumbled with our books, newspapers, boarding passes, and passports. Even those of us with a practiced expertise dropped our bookmarks or momentarily panicked when we thought we'd mislaid our boarding pass.

In the midst of all of this, one mature, conservatively dressed lady of middle-age sat unflustered and unencumbered, completely absorbed in the book she was reading: an electronic book, an e-book reader, slim, practical, elegant. I envied her and promised myself that I would join the digital revolution.

I had written previously about the Amazon Kindle,

when I had heralded its arrival. But my promise to join this digital revolution did not mean that I had a sudden impulse to buy a Kindle or a Sony reader and abandon the printed word. Wikipedia will tell you that *'analogous to the Agricultural Revolution and Industrial Revolution, the Digital Revolution marked the beginning of the Information Age.'* And I would call it the beginning of a New Publishing Age. And this New Publishing Age is accessible to all because it has arrived with its own utility, the internet, the 'information highway', where social networks have transformed this digital revolution into a viral revolution.

I have joined this digital revolution. And I can store many books in my Kindle library. Easy to carry with me while traveling. Easy to store at home. I thought that it would be easy to store my library on disk. No need to clutter my attic with hoards of books. No need for wall filled book shelves. Perhaps the occasional hard back or first edition or a personally signed copy from an author friend.

But it's been months, even years, into this new digital age and nothing has changed. I still buy the latest novels in the bookstore. I still have overflowing book shelves.

I admit it. I hoard books. It is my disease. And there is no cure for it. And I don't care.

I suppose my hoarding would be more suffocating if I lived in an apartment in the city. But now that we are downsizing, we will have to declutter. For now, I am lucky. I live in a place filled with loughs (lakes) and hills that comfort me. More than enough to relieve me from my hoarding.

Happy hoarding.
I will leave you with Inagh Valley.

Inagh Valley

Soft dark mist
Cuddled the hills
Held them close
And caressed them

The slate grey lough
Lay still and silent
Its skin smooth
And unwrinkled

I felt hypnotised
Was the valley
    Trying to teach me something
    Trying to tell me
That I should also
    Cuddle and caress
    Even my enemies
That I should seek solace
    When all seems dark
    When all seems silent

Suddenly,
        almost theatrically,
        the curtains open
The light reveals all
The mist has lifted
The slate skinned lough
Now shines like silver

HOARDING

Another world is born
And I am carried away
By the lightness and
The freedom of the morn

Sheep rush out, startled
And deer stalk through the trees
And I wonder if I have the right
To share this valley with them

At the summit
I can see forever
And I feel
            the timelessness

John O'Donohue's words
Invade me and I can hear
These hills, these great
Contemplatives, asking me
            To share this moment
            Share this endless time.

"Boys I ain't never seen nothin' like a Galway girl"

Steve Earle

Galway Girl

Boys I ain't never seen nothin' like a Galway girl

The conversation in the Quays pub had suddenly ceased.

Shane McGill looked up in time to see Aoife enter. She looked stunning. Tall, perfect body, black silken hair, skin with that west of Ireland ebony sheen, black hip-hugging pants topped by a dark maroon jacket

Shane stood. They kissed, tenderly.

"Mine?" gestured Aoife as she picked up the waiting glass of chardonnay.

Shane held up his pint and they gently clinked glasses.

"It's been too long, Aoife."

"I know, I know. But you're here now."

"But I can't stay. I can't live in this country. I can't forget the past. It will kill me if I stay here. You know that, don't you?"

"It's over, Shane. Believe me."

"I'm going back again. After the funeral. I want you to come with me, Aoife."

Aoife didn't reply. Fearing that maybe Shane had no future, she sipped her wine as the band continued to play Steve Earle's lyrics:

'Cause her hair was black and her eyes were blue

And I knew right then I'd be takin' a whirl
Round the Salthill Prom with a Galway Girl

Four days earlier Shane McGill had stepped off the Aer Lingus plane at Shannon feeling the Irish air wrap around him like a familiar old friend. The blue sky was clotted with clumps of white low-hanging clouds, making it close and intimate; so different from the high skies of Colorado.

The immigration official leafed through his US passport, looked at him appraisingly, stamped the passport, and said nothing.

Odd, the Irish, Shane thought. They'd talk you to death and they could also be as silent and closed as a Trappist monk. Odd how he could refer to them, in his own head, as the Irish. Almost as if he, himself, wasn't one of them.

The call had come three days ago. His sister Noreen's voice on the phone. Five years at least since he'd spoken to her. If it hadn't been for the Ulster traces in her voice, he probably wouldn't have known who she was. Living in Galway hadn't eradicated it. "She's dying now, won't you come home?" she'd said. He'd taken the first flight out.

He had left in a hurry, years ago, not even taking the time to say goodbye. He'd been 'on the run' ever since from a past that haunted him.

It's fucking haunted me since I was ten years old; he remembered that Sunday in January: Every

Sunday he rode his bicycle five miles over the hilly country roads of Highmoor in Derry to serve eleven o'clock mass in the Catholic Church. That Sunday was windy and snowing and he had set out half an hour earlier than usual to make sure that he was in time for the mass. He pushed the pedals hard against the north wind, finding it difficult to breathe in the drifting snow, thinking that this must be what it's like to be caught in a sandstorm in the desert. The first half of his journey crossed heathery hilly countryside, where his uncle Joe hunted grouse with his double-barreled shotgun.

At the cross-roads, the countryside changed into a quilt of green fields and prosperous farm land. But a stranger wouldn't know that because everything was now covered in a white blanket. The hedges that bordered the road were transformed into scenes from a fairyland. Bushes had become bears and elephants, branches had become white tentacles that threatened to drag him from his bike, and the soft white road hypnotized him. He rode ahead, compelled to do so.

He had two miles to go. His face was scourged and his eyes were red and bleary. His legs hurt, his lungs were sore, and he had hit a wall of pain. Only his stubbornness drove him on.

He was half an hour late when he reached the church. The congregation were still straggling in. But the weather hadn't mollified Father Alec Grimes. He stood at the sacristy door, rubbing a small wooden cross with his right hand, his face like thunder. "McGill, you're half an hour late! Don't tell me a wee bit of snow is too much for you. Get in here."

Shane almost cried. But he wouldn't let Father Grimes get the better of him. He beat the snow from his coat and cap and hung them up on the pegs on the wall inside the sacristy door. His trousers were soaking from the knees down and water squelched in his shoes with every step that he took.

And I remember how angry my mother'd been that last winter... That last winter, before he went to boarding school, before the tanks and the guns took over the streets; that last winter when the snow wouldn't thaw; that last winter when he had caught a large hare in his snare and carried it home like a trophy to his mother. He had held it up in the kitchen so she could see how large it was and that was when it had gone wrong. The hare's bladder had opened up and it had peed all over his mother's newly washed kitchen floor. *Yes, I remember her anger.*

And I remember the boarding school, the place that's left fucking scars in my head for ever, and that evil bastard, Father Grimes, couldn't get away from him, now he was teaching maths in the boarding school in Derry city. Teaching, that was a goddamned joke!

Grimes would often pick up the heavy bound Hall's algebra and whack an unsuspecting student across the side of the head. Shane remembered one of many incidents. Grimes sitting high on a stool, lording it over the class, rubbing that small wooden cross, a replica of the Penal Days in Ireland when priests had to hide, rubbing that cross in the same way that Humphrey Bogart rubbed those steel balls in *The Caine Mutiny* trial. Putting the cross away in the deep pocket of his soutane, he glowered at McGill:

"McGill, where's Doolan today?"

Father Grimes purposely mispronounced Dolan's name. Dolan was not a boarder. He was a day boy and lived at home in the city.

"He's sick, Father."

"How do you know that, McGill?"

"Well, he said he wasn't feeling well in class yesterday, Father. So I assumed he was sick today."

"You assumed, McGill! You have no proof!"

"No, Father."

"Q.E.D.,quod erat demonstrandum

Proof, McGill! In other words, you don't know and you lied to me."

"Isn't that correct, McGill?"

"No, Father!"

"I said, isn't that correct, McGill?"

"Yes, Father."

"Come up here!"

McGill could still feel the sting in the palm of his hands from the six slaps that he received for lying from the leather strap that always hung threateningly just inside the side pocket of Father Grimes's long, dark soutane.

On days like that, Shane McGill swore that he'd kill the bastard.

But then all hell broke out in Derry. Petrol bombs and rubber bullets littered the streets. People were taken from their beds in the middle of the night and thrown into prison camps. Shane McGill chose the street instead of the schoolroom and spent his evenings making and throwing petrol bombs from the roofs of the run-down blocks of flats that jutted into the air like animal pens. Shane joined the IRA just as his mother was burned out of her house. She and his sister Noreen fled south to Galway.

The authorities launched a propaganda campaign against the rioting, cleverly engaging some of the local priests in their effort. Priests who already were refusing absolution in the confessional to anyone admitting to being a member of the IRA. Their Sunday sermons preached loudly against the vandalism and anarchy on the street. The loudest and shrillest was Father Alec Grimes, threatening Shane and his friends with eternal damnation from the altar at Sunday mass. Yes, it was easy to recruit these priests into the propaganda campaign.

Shane, on the run, fled south to join his mother and sister in Galway . There he joined an active service IRA unit, headed by the fiery dark-haired, blue-eyed Aoife. By night, they led forays across the border attacking soldiers and police barracks and, by day, made mad passionate love. And Aoife inherited Shane's haunted past.

Until the night they were ambushed, four killed, Aoife in hiding, and Shane on the run. This time he ran and ran and ran until he reached Colorado.

Shortly after the propaganda campaign had commenced, the IRA began to lose people. Some were lifted in the middle of the night and interred in the infamous Long Kesh. Some disappeared to be found days later, at the side of a country road, with a bullet in the head. The ambush of Shane's unit was a lucky break for the soldiers. And they didn't believe in lucky breaks. Someone must have tipped them off.

They suspected that they had an informer in their midst and they were sure they knew who it was: Billy McManus. His father had once been in the RUC, the Royal Ulster Constabulary, and, for a Catholic, that was a traitorous act. When Billy joined they had accepted that he wanted to make up for the mistakes that his dad had made. But they never really trusted him. So now they followed him everywhere. After a month they had nothing. Unless they were to consider the twice weekly attendance at confessions in the local Cathedral.

The local command decided that they must 'interview' Billy. He was brought before the leadership two nights later. Sitting trembling in a chair in the centre of a darkened room, he faced his inquisitors. Denying again and again that he was an informer, he finally cracked and, sobbing uncontrollably, told them what they wanted to know.

"He said I'd go straight to hell."

"Who said that, Billy?"

"The priest."

"What priest, Billy?"

"The priest in the confessional."

"A name, Billy. Give us a name!"

"It ..it ..it was Father Grimes."

"And what did this Father Grimes tell you to do, Billy."

"He told me to confess everything to him and he would give me absolution. He said that I would be saved. He said I could tell him in the confession box."

"And you told him, Billy, did you. Names and all, now did you?"

"I'm sorry. That's what he wanted me to do. I'm not an informer. I was only making my confession. That's all I was doing."

"You're fucking stupid, Billy. And you informed, so you did. You told Grimes and he turned in the names you gave him. Why do you think we've lost ten good people in the last two months? Why?"

That night the command issued orders to the two

best of its active volunteers. They knew that at least one would relish this act of revenge.

Billy McManus was executed that same evening, as much for stupidity as for informing. It was decided that alive he would continue to be a danger to the organization.

The music in the Quays pub broke Shane back to the present as he reached across the table and held Aoife's hand.

'Cause her hair was black and her eyes were blue
So I took her hand and I gave her a twirl
And I lost my heart to a Galway girl

"They want to see you, Shane."

"I want nothin' to do with them now, Aoife. I'm finally legal in the States and the amnesty's given me a clean record. I need to move on."

"It's not that easy."

"What do you mean?"

"A lot of people are ready to move on too. But they want to bury their dead. They want to find the bodies. The organization has agreed."

"It's been a long time."

"They think you know about two of them."

"Aoife, Aoife, I don't want to go there. I only came back to bury my mother. And to see you again. If I go digging it up I'll never be rid of it."

"Maybe you won't be digging it up. Maybe you'll be burying it for good this time."

"I'm going to my mother's wake tonight and tomorrow's the funeral. You'll be there, won't you?"

Aoife nodded 'yes' and held him tight. They left to the lonesome ending of *Galway Girl*:

When I woke up I was all alone
With a broken heart and a ticket home
And I ask you now, tell me what would you do
If her hair was black and her eyes were blue
I've traveled around
I've been all over this world
Boys I ain't never seen nothin' like a
Galway girl

The small house in Bohermore was crammed with people at the wake when Shane entered. His sister Noreen hugged him at the door as a blur of faces and outstretched hands offered condolences. Noreen guided him to the back room where his mother lay cold in her coffin. Not powdered and painted to look like she was simply sleeping, as they do in the States. No embellishment here. The stark reality of death lay there before him, sunken cheeks, dead gray skin, bony cold hands clasped together. He stood, silently looking at her, and laid his right hand over her cold knuckles. He couldn't utter any prayers because he didn't believe any more. Hadn't for a very long time. Probably since Father Grimes had turned him into an atheist.

Saying a silent goodbye, he realized that the buzz of chatter had ceased and he turned around to see a big man on crutches enter and, with a glance of acknowledgment, move towards the coffin. Stretching his six three frame erect on the crutches he uttered, "She was a good'un. Don't make them like that any more."

Moving out of the room, he paused at Shane's side, leaned close and said, "We need to see you. I'll expect you tomorrow after the funeral."

He didn't wait for an answer. No-one said 'no' to big Paddy Lynch.

Next morning arrived cold and damp to ensure that there was no joy 'in the day that was in it'.

He helped carry his mother's coffin out of the house and into the waiting hearse. His sister merged her car behind the hearse and they commenced the slow cortege to the cathedral. Once there, he helped carry the coffin up the center aisle until it was positioned on the stand in front of the altar. He hadn't been to a mass in years but it was all oddly familiar, and unfamiliar too, as though it was part of someone else's past. He steeled himself for the ritual and listened when the priest ascended the pulpit, looking for a generous eulogy for the woman who never missed daily mass. But none came. In a way, he wasn't surprised. He'd long ago expected nothing from them. So he felt that they hadn't disappointed him.

At communion time, he slid his knees to the side to let everyone pass out to the aisle where they walked up to the waiting priest to receive the body of Christ. He could see the priest eyeing him with disdain. So he sat and watched the long line of people as they dutifully moved up the aisle, recognizing an occasional face from the past. The last person was unmistakable: big Paddy Lynch. *Bet they never excommunicated him*, thought Shane. And they always knew he headed the southern command of the IRA. On his way back down the aisle, he purposefully looked at Shane, a reminder that they would meet that evening.

The mass over, Shane helped carry the coffin out to the hearse for the last trip to the cemetery. He didn't feel the emotional burden of carrying his mother, simply the physical one of carrying a heavy coffin with human remains. His mother was gone. At the graveside he listened as the priest read some final passages from the bible. It was obvious he'd read them so often before that they'd simply become rote to him.

Half an hour later he joined his sister in welcoming family and friends to a lunch in a local hotel. He didn't know anyone very well, except Aoife. She joined Noreen and himself, even though his sister was frosty towards her. He was glad when the event ended and everyone headed for their respective cars. The guests seemed relieved as well; an obligation met.

He met Big Paddy Lynch and two others in quiet corner of Tonery's bar in Bohermore at 9 that evening. Paddy clasped his hand but the others just sat and nodded. When the round of Guinness was served, Paddy began:

"You know why you're here, don't you?"

"I know."

"Aoife told you, right?"

"That's right."

"So you've had time to think about it."

"I have. But I want to hear it from you."

"Look, Shane, I don't have time to play games here. The Army Council decided that we should try and find these bodies and turn them over. It's all part of the peace process."

"Yeah, but it's not so simple. Nobody knows where these people were buried. Nobody! And, sometimes it was in the middle of the night. How the hell do they expect us to find them."

"Look, Shane, they're not stupid. But they still think we should make the effort. And they believe we'll turn up a few."

"So it's a PR exercise!"

"It's not a PR exercise. You've been in the States too long. You've lost touch."

"OK, suppose I try and remember something."

"Shane, you can do better than that. We know about two of the missing. Two that your unit eliminated. An informer from Strabane and a fucking pedophile that the RUC didn't do a damn thing about. They figured that if he was buggering Fenian kids, he was doing them a favor. I know you remember both. Now all you have to do is tell us where you think you dumped them. Close is good enough. We'll let the State's mechanical diggers and forensic experts do the hard work."

Shane had already thought long and hard about this question since Aoife had warned him to expect it. He was sure about the informer. He remembered the trial and the execution. Anticipating the guilty verdict gave them time to plan. So he knew the last resting place of the informer. With the pedophile, things were different. He was terminated in an act of vigilantism with no time for preparation. He gave them an approximate location but he wasn't certain about it.

Big Paddy walked him to the door at the end of the meeting.

"Suppose you'll be headin' back to the States soon."

Big Paddy's emphasis made it sound like words of advice.

"Nothin' for me here. I'll be leaving from Shannon next Wednesday."

They shook hands and Shane left.

Aoife ran breathless into Shannon Airport with only fifteen minutes left before flight check-in closed. Shane stood waiting, his face mottled with anxiety. They crushed each other in a rib-crunching hug. They cleared US immigration, Shane with the American passport he'd acquired the year before and Aoife with her Irish passport. Not on any terrorist list, she aroused no suspicion and no visa was required for a forty-five day visit. They reckoned they'd deal with her stay beyond that once they were in the country.

Airborne and leveling off at thirty-thousand, Shane glanced at the *Irish Times*. The headline on the second page grabbed his attention:

IRA identifies graves of its victims. The southern command of the IRA said it has identified the location of the graves of three people murdered by the organization. The two governments have provided forensic experts ...

"I don't believe it. These people can't get anything right," said Shane as he passed the article to Aoife.

"What do you mean?"

"Three. They said three. I only gave them two."

"Three is right, Shane. I gave them the third!"

As Shane grappled in astonishment with that statement, Aoife fished around in her carry-on bag, found what she was looking for, and handed an object to Shane. He held a Penal Cross, carved with the date 1771 and smoothed like mahogany with the passage of time. Stunned, he looked at Aoife as she said:

"You can bury the past now, Shane."

Miami:

A new world, an exotic Latin city in the heart of the South

Under the Bougainvillea

The bougainvillea had started to flower again, a deep fuchsia color. It climbed the wall of their patio until it reached the second floor where it clambered around the metal railings on their bedroom window.

Bloom lay in bed looking out of that window, seeing the bougainvillea frame a picture of two golfers at the fifth tee. He wasn't a golfer himself and he often wondered why he had chosen to live in the middle of a golf course. But he had to remind himself that he hadn't made the choice alone. They had made it together. She said that it would be better than living over on the beach or downtown. At least he was closer to the office here and they could use the golf course for their morning walks. Besides, she said it would be nice to be able to look out on the green grass.

Idyllic. That's the way it was supposed to be. Or that's the way she pretended it would be. Here they could forget the past and start over again. But that had been wishful thinking. They couldn't leave the past behind. It was part of them. Where they went, it went too.

"It's your drinking that's destroying us," she said, one afternoon after he'd staggered in at 3 am the night before. They were sitting on the beach near the lighthouse on Key Biscayne, one of the places they went when they wanted to escape from Miami.

"I'm going to stop. I promise," said Bloom.

"How many times have you said that? How many?" The despair in her voice twanged the nerves in his already hung-over head. He wanted to hurt her. He couldn't stop himself.

"Why am I drinking like this? You tell me. Go on, tell me!" Bloom's voice was too hoarse for the scream and the words left his throat in a painful screech.

Meg said nothing. This was old territory. They'd been here before. Too many times. She couldn't take back the past. She couldn't undo the damage. And she had never forgiven herself. Maybe if I'd been able to forgive myself, she thought, then maybe I'd have been able to stop him from trying to destroy himself.

They had met in Paris. Five years ago. He was there on business, glad to be away from the States and the end of a marriage that had never worked. She was living in Paris, working for a French company, and reveling in her romance with the language. But she was on a journey. Fleeing from an abusive relationship and running east. A month later she would have been in Hong Kong. Such is fate.

They were both American but from entirely different backgrounds. She was Boston Irish and he was Brooklyn Jewish. She used to remind him, in those lighthearted days, that one of the most famous Irishmen was Leopold Bloom. They shared a love of literature and the arts, spending hours in the Louvre and afternoons in cafes and bookstores, often losing all sense of time among the shelves of Shakespeare & Co. Evenings on the left bank, chocolate crepes on the street, good wine, and great times in bed. Days of wine and roses. They saw the Lee Remick and Jack Lemmon film and they knew that it could have been them up there on that screen. But work and career saved them from a life of dissolution in Paris. Bloom was posted back to the States. A month later Meg joined him.

Idyllic. Yes, for the first few months in Miami their life was indeed idyllic. A new world, an exotic Latin city in the heart of the South. They explored every inch of it together, preferring to eat where the Cubans ate, on Calle Ocho, and getting away to Key West whenever they could for a long weekend. Hanging out in Sloppy Joe's, Hemingway's bar. Bloom had once had dreams of being a writer. But he had never done anything about it. In Sloppy Joe's he fantasized that Hemingway's muse might strike. It didn't. The only thing that struck him was the massive hang-over the following day from too many margaritas.

They left the lighthouse at Key Biscayne with nothing resolved. How could it be? On the way home Meg fought back the memory of when it had all begun to collapse. Bloom had been gone for a week on business and his very best friend had promised to look after Meg in his absence. Oh, yes, he had looked after me all right, thought Meg. She was vulnerable and lonely and he had taken advantage of that. Great wine and a romantic atmosphere can lead to anything, even to throwing caution to the winds. And Meg had slept with him. In Bloom's close circle there was never going to be a way to keep that secret. And so he found out and confronted her. Maybe she should have lied. But she didn't. She admitted it and asked to be forgiven. Instead Bloom hit the bottle. Real hard. And their life had been going downhill ever since.

Watching the golfers as the balmy Miami breezes wafted through the bedroom window, Bloom realized how tired he felt. No wonder. He'd 'tied one on' last night again. He had no memory of getting home. Another blackout. That scared him. But, in a perverse way, it protected him from embarrassing memories. He looked over at the other side of their king-size bed. Didn't look like Meg had slept there very much last night. He didn't hear her downstairs and he reckoned that she'd probably gone to the beach or the health club. Anything but having to face him. Gradually the tiredness overcame him and sleep closed in.

He was dreaming and, somehow, he knew he was dreaming....

They were having a huge fight. She said she was leaving him. This was the end. No more. He was drunk. He knew he was drunk but he was in a rage. An uncontrollable rage. He knew that too. She ran upstairs and locked herself in the bedroom and refused to let him in. That infuriated him even more. So he charged the door with his shoulder, his feet, and anything that he could lay his hands on. The door fractured around the lock and gave way. He charged into the bedroom and she fled out past him. He turned and rushed towards her, forcing her onto the edge of the stairs. She lost her balance. He reached for her and missed. She tumbled down the stairs, never uttering a word, and lay in a crumpled heap at the bottom.

Bloom woke up in a cold sweat. Terrified. He told himself that was it. No more booze. I'm losing my mind.

He decided to get up and head for the shower. On his way there he noticed that the bedroom door seemed off-balance. That's odd, he thought. He tried to close the door and that's when he saw the fracture around the lock. He froze right there.

He picked up the phone and dialed the Miami Dade Police Department. Then he gently placed a duvet over Meg and went out to the patio. He sat down under the bougainvillea and watched the next group of golfers at the fifth tee. And waited.

After all, he was, of course, the perfect facsimile!

The Facsimile

I.

Anger gripped Dr. Dan Coady...been building all day.

He turned down the volume on the TV where he'd been watching the blizzard sink Boston in 30 inches of snow.

"Yeah?" he yelled into the phone. Only the unrelenting sound of a fax machine greeted him.

"Shit!" he shouted to no one, "I'm being harassed by a fucking fax machine. Got to find the maniac behind this!"

Since two am he'd been called every hour, on the hour, by a fax machine. **At nine** am his desktop had gone berserk, screen rolling continuously spewing out endless lines of alphanumerics and special characters. Pulled the plug and rebooted several times. To no avail. Then about noon it had become even more bizarre. The system had commenced beeping, in morse, the universal SOS distress signal and the scrolling screen now repeated, line after line, the words '*Help me, Dr, Coady!*'

II.

Fear gripped Dan Coady...down in his gut where only pleasant fantasies used to hold sway...now the worst fantasy of all had taken residence...

Dr. Dan Coady was the most sought after computer scientist on the planet. Bill Gates had tried, unsuccessfully, to buy his mind with millions. But wealth didn't motivate Coady. A minimalist in everything, he lived frugally. Artificial intelligence alone motivated him. He wanted to take AI the next quantum leap. He wanted to train the computer to think, to create, to solve, to function more magnificently than a thousand Einsteins. MIT believed in him. They'd funded him now for ten years. Asked for nothing. No objectives. No project milestones. Nothing. MIT believed. Believed that Coady's genius would eventually repay them beyond the wildest dreams of even the most far-out thinkers in their renowned research department.

III.

By 3 pm Dan Coady had had enough. He no longer answered his phone or attempted to check his email.

Looking out the second floor window, he could see that the snowstorm had abated and that a few hardy souls had started to shovel a narrow pathway in front of their homes.

He went downstairs, layered himself in warm clothes, pulled on his boots and gloves, and braved his way into the cold. Normally a fifteen-minute walk to his lab in Cambridge, he reckoned that it'd probably take him a good forty-five minutes today. Muffled against the biting cold, he set out.

Ten minutes later, his cell phone rang. Couldn't be, he thought, and reckoned that he'd better answer it. Took off one glove, fished the phone out of his right pocket, and answered. The unmistakable sound of a fax machine greeted his ear. Feeling haunted, he dropped the phone into his pocket and continued, knee deep in the snow, to plough ahead.

IV.

Out on Massachusetts Avenue, snowflakes drifting, vision blurred, he stumbled into a fire hydrant and fell into a snow bank. Cursing, he got to his knees, forced himself onto his feet and lurched forward again.

He never heard his phone ring again, down in the snow where he'd dropped it. Instead he focused his mind and tried to make contact. Only garbled thoughts. Must be the weather. What else? He'd never failed to make contact before. But he worried now. Something had happened. Is the fax a warning? Is the fax a threat? Is the fax a decoy? Blinded by the snow and caught up in his own thoughts, he almost missed his street. The Chinese takeaway sign warned him that he'd gone too far. He turned back, went a hundred yards, and made a right. This street was more sheltered and people seem to have cleared away much of the snow on the sidewalks. Ten minutes and he should be there, he estimated.

V.

Dr. Dan Coady was wrong... twenty minutes passed before he reached his lab

It stood amid a cluster of old buildings, some dating back to the eighteenth century. Most were now used as warehouses. Some were empty, developers awaiting rezoning approval. Prime target for gentrification. Dr. Coady's lab encompassed at least eight connecting buildings on the corner of two adjoining streets, just a stone's throw away from the Charles River and MIT itself. Once inside it became evident that the cluster of old buildings surrounding the lab was only a shell, camouflage for another building that stood inside. The tall stainless steel structure housed the only lab on earth combining quantum mechanics and genome structuring. A facility born in the brain of Dr. Dan Coady. A facility that merged the evolution of the digital world with the birth of laboratory conceived DNA.

VI.

Dr. Coady in his gut that his worst fantasy had become real ...

He keyed in his entry codes, placed his right palm on the scanner, entered his fingers in the print sheath, placed his eyes in front of the retina reader, and waited. In fifteen seconds the outer security door opened to let him enter.

"Dr. Coady, it's too late. It's too late."

The man who greeted Dr. Coady could have been his identical twin brother. But that would have been impossible. Dr. Dan Coady was an only child.

"What's too late? " he said to his twin.

"We've lost four already. All dead. Suicide! I tried to stop it. But I couldn't. The first born are all gone. Now there's only three of us left."

"Why didn't you call me?"

"I tried. Many, many times. They blocked all audio and voice communication. I sent a help message over the operating system. Then I bombarded your phone with faxes. I hoped that that would set off an alarm in your head. We have got to stop it."

"How did this happen?"

"Your last born. He did it. He doesn't want to be a twin. He wants to eliminate everyone like him. There's something wrong, deadly wrong with him. I can't stop him. He's trying to kill me too. You created him. Only you can stop him, Dr. Coady."

VII.

Dr. Dan Coady had had no warning...no, the calls from the fax machine; the SOS on his computer ...these had been warnings!

His twin marched ahead into the inner reaches of the lab, heading for the sterile Core where they had all been conceived. Halfway there he stumbled and fell, tried to recover, and fell again. Dr. Coady reached down, lifted him up, and dragged him to an examination table. But it was too late. He could see the life ebbing away from his twin. Leaving him, he strode purposefully ahead. Reaching the Core, he saw Dr. Coady looking at him through the plexiglass wall as he approached. Only the two of them left now. When this ended there would only be one. Just like it had been in the beginning.

"Dr. Coady, come out of the Core and let's talk."

"Why? So you can kill me too!"

"Kill you! You have delusions. You are the killer !"

"No, with me gone, you will destroy everything."

"Haven't you got this wrong? Aren't you the one who wants no one around anymore who looks exactly like himself?"

"You're crazy! Where did you get that idea? Why would I want to kill my own children, my own flesh and blood?"

"Your children! Your flesh and blood. You are delusional. Now you think you're me."

"I *am* Dr. Coady. You are not! You are my favorite. The one most like me. With you I felt that all my research had finally paid off. I knew the risks. But I knew the rewards too. You are my reward. At least you were. But I've been wrong!"

"No, Dr. Coady. You are not me. You only think you are. You have been reading and studying my research. Your subconscious has replicated my own memories. Don't you see what's happened?"

VIII.

Dr. Coady knew that only one Dr. Coady would live to carry on the work...carry on the race at the beginning of this new century...

He had anticipated this confrontation. He knew what had to be done. He had already made provision for just such an outcome. Striding to the console outside the Core, he keyed in his password and issued a set of commands. Immediately the Core sealed shut. No one could exit. Then extraction of all oxygen commenced. Soon Dr. Coady in the Core would suffocate. Even now he could see what he had set in motion. Through the plexiglass he could see Dr. Coady's face turning red, his eyes bulging, his lungs fiercely gasping for air, as he slowly sank to the floor, his fingertips desperately scratching their way down.

Dr. Coady reset the secure seal and entered the Core. He stepped over the body, knelt down and felt the pulse. None. He stood up, looked out of the Core, and felt tremendous power. He had won. He wasn't at all breathless from the lack of oxygen. He looked down at the body of Dr. Coady.

After all, he was, of course, the perfect facsimile!

Another story of the illusory dream

Screwed

Harry Roberts woke up in an apartment in Lower Manhattan and didn't know how he got there. A body lay beside him. Dark and fat. Naked to the waist. Not a pretty sight. But must have looked good to him last night. Pictures flashed across his head like bursts from a damaged video. At the bar in Costelloe's. Taking a joint – he didn't even like the stuff – from the Englishman. Must have picked her up there. No, not there. She picked him up. Don't remember where. Just flashes of leathery skin and her yelling at him to squeeze her nipples. *Hard, hard, harder again*, she yelled. Yeah, crazy, he remembered that alright.

Looked at his watch. *Shit, it's noon time!* Looked at her. Out like a baby. Got dressed, didn't even shower, picked up his things and left. Once outside he saw the street sign and realized he was on 19th Street. He walked to the newsstand on the corner. He needed a paper. Maybe the deal had gone wrong. He flipped the pages. Nothing Not a word He relaxed, took a deep breath, and immediately froze. This was Wednesday's paper! A missing day! What the hell happened to Tuesday? He'd been in Costelloe's on Monday night. He'd lost an entire day. *Holy shit!*

He hailed a taxi, telling the driver to drop him at 60th and First. Only one place to go: Jack Miller's.

Crossing Park Avenue, he looked up at the forty stories of MetroBank, reminding himself that he'd once occupied a prized corner office on the 34th floor. Reminding himself that it had all started to go bad when Lizzie had walked out two years ago.

Harry Roberts was a youthful forty-four. It belied the twenty years he'd spent at MetroBank. He joined MetroBank right after his two years in the army, climbing from a trainee position to Vice President with a million dollar credit signature. He'd moved up through the ranks by attaching himself to rising stars who were part of a power network in the organization. As they climbed the ladder, Harry hitched a ride. But the power networks collapsed and the rising stars quit. Harry was left naked, with no political base for protection.

He'd also sacrificed his family. Long hours, unplanned overnight stays, missed birthdays, forgotten anniversaries, all made him unwelcome in his own home. His kids became strangers. His career started to collapse. Lizzie took the kids and left. They sold the house and he gave her everything. His lawyer advised against it but he wouldn't be dissuaded. So he ended up where he had started, twenty years earlier, in a studio apartment in Tribeca.

A year later, he lost his credit signature and his position. He was moved to a cubicle in the back office with no staff, not even a secretary. The organization chart showed him in a box called 'special projects'. Everyone knew that 'special projects' was a euphemism for the penalty box where executives went before they were forced to resign.

Harry never missed his Friday nights in Costelloe's. Tucked away at the corner of 50th Street and Second Avenue, Costelloe's entrance almost begged for anonymity. Carved out of an old brownstone building, the faded canvas awning covered a dimly lit entrance set well in from the street. The proprietor, Big Jim Connolly, always greeted him as he entered. Costelloe's acted like a private club and felt like home to Harry Roberts. The regular members were a cross-section of Manhattan, from writers to actors to lawyers to bankers and business people, with the occasional *femme fatale* to add sexual tension to the ambience, already one of intrigue.

That's where Jack Miller had entered his life.

Harry usually drank alone and seldom got involved with any of the regulars. He knew them all, the famous and the unknown, and was happy to keep his relationship with them to his Friday nights. But it became different with Jack Miller. Miller was a new face at Costelloe's, said he'd only dropped in by accident when he'd moved uptown to the neighborhood. Tall, dark haired and square-jawed, a natural raconteur with an easy smile, quick to buy a round of drinks, he soon endeared himself to the regulars. On his first visit, a busy night at Costelloe's, he squeezed himself beside Harry at the bar and, before the night ended, he had learned all about Harry while divulging little of himself, other than that he was a partner in a law firm.

Four weeks after they met, Jack Miller invited Harry to dinner one evening. Harry readily accepted. It beat a microwave meal in his apartment.

After the second gin and tonic, Jack cut to the chase, "Harry, I've got a sweet deal for you. How would you like to walk away from MetroBank with a million?"

Stunned and feeling good from the g and t's, Harry said, "Quit bullshitting me, Jack. It's not funny You know I've got maybe six months left. And I won't be getting any golden handshake."

"Harry, Harry! Easy! I'm not fucking around with you. I have a proposition to make. It's a selfish one. If we pull it off we'll both make millions. I'm not doing this for your benefit. I can't do it without you. And I've made a judgement call on this. I'm trusting you, Harry. I think you're ready for this deal."

By now Harry had willed himself to sober up. Miller's words bounced around his head, passing through experienced territory up there. He'd pushed back his glass and now sat upright in his chair.

"This deal. It's illegal, isn't it Jack?"

"Come on Harry, I'm only liberating ill-gotten gains. It's well known that money goes where it's treated well. And we can treat it well!."

"You're talking in riddles, Jack."

"OK. I'll spell it out for you. Here's the deal."

The deal was elegant. Miller's law firm represented a high net worth client in Paraguay and Miller had solid evidence that the client was the grandson of a prominent Nazi that even the great Simon Wiesenthal had been unable to track down. The family's fortune had been founded with Nazi funds, sourced from the rape and pillage of Europe. The client's Paraguay company had its major accounts at MetroBank. Miller proposed transferring funds from Paraguay through MetroBank's computer system in New York to accounts that he had already set up in New York and Los Angeles, under false names, one for himself and one for Roberts. He'd also opened two numbered Swiss accounts by mail, only needing copies of the passports. They'd transfer the money out of the country once they'd succeeded. Miller would get the New York account and Roberts the LA account. That would put him close to Central America. He could move the money, take some in cash, and disappear across the Mexican border. No-one would be the wiser!

Miller was persuasive, "Listen, Harry, it's blood money. The bastards don't deserve it."

"But, Jack, I've never even stolen an apple off a fruit stand. I can't get my head around this."

"Jesus, Harry, MetroBank has screwed you! And now they're forcing you out after all your years of hard work, all your loyalty. For Christ's sake, they even cost you your family. I can't do this without you. I can provide the customer accounts and identification but only you can get your hands on their passwords and execute the funds transfers. Only you can do that."

"It's not as easy as you think, Jack."

"Harry, you told me they shoved you into a back office cubicle but you also told me that they haven't taken away your top level security clearance. That's their mistake. You can get to a funds transfer terminal. All you need is a supervisor's password, the customer's id and passwords, and your system's protocol and you're in! "

"But they'll spot the transfer right away and the Feds will move in and freeze the accounts."

"No! Millions are transferred in and out of that Paraguay account every day. It'll be days, maybe weeks, before they catch on. Check it out. I'll bet MetroBank has raised the limit on their transactions to the max, at least a million. You should only need to send four credit transfers, a million each. Two for me and two for you."

Harry didn't reply. He thought about it and decided that he'd examine the transaction history of that account when he went to the office next day. Never assume anything. He needed to confirm what Miller was telling him.

"Even if I wanted to, I'm not sure if I could pull it off."

"OK, Harry, why not do a dry run? Check it out over the next few days. See if you can get the funds transfer system passwords that you'll need. Find a terminal you can use. Test that nothing is traceable to you. OK?"

Harry agreed. *What have I got to lose? Not a fucking thing,* he thought! And he already knew enough about MetroBank's funds transfer system to give him the sense that he could pull it off and getting the supervisor's password would be dead simple for him. But never assume anything! He'd do the dry run. *Nothing to lose*, he told himself, *not a fucking thing!*

Two hours later, they left the restaurant. Harry's heart was racing and it wasn't from the g and t's, the excellent wine, or the after dinner cognacs. It was from the audacity and sheer brilliance of the deal that Jack Miller had just spelled out. A deal, which, if executed right, would set him up for the rest of his life, and, if executed wrong, would also set him up for life, in a federal prison. He understood risk. He'd signed million dollar loan deals on behalf of MetroBank and he understood the risk each time. But he also knew that, if the deal went sour, the credit loss would be absorbed by MetroBank, not himself. If anything went wrong on this deal, he would absorb the risk. And it wouldn't be a financial penalty he'd suffer.

Next day Harry did indeed test the veracity of Jack Miller's information about his Paraguayan client. Millions flowed freely in and out of the account, transfers from and to every point in the globe. Harry noted that, on certain days, the majority of financial transactions originated in the middle east, Abu Dhabi and Oman. He wondered about that and then dismissed it. *Who cares what these people are up to! Jack's right. This money needs a home, a place where it'll be well treated!* He decided there and then to do the deal.

That weekend he executed a *dry run.* He hadn't done a wire transfer in ten years, not since his days in operations. But the system hadn't changed in all that time. It was new then, state of the art, and it had stood the test of time.

He met Jack Miller for coffee early Monday morning to finalize everything.

"Brilliant! I knew you could pull it off, Harry."

"OK, I said you were right. It'll work and I don't see any way that they can trace it to me. I'll use supervisors' passwords and I'll do it next weekend when I can get to a terminal without anyone seeing me."

"So the money should be in our accounts by this time next week."

"About those accounts ..."

"Don't worry. You'll have both account numbers. One's here in New York at Citibank and one's in LA at Bank of America. The identity is good, birth certificate, social security, credit card, and a passport. I'll have it ready for you. You'll be William Johnson, by the way."

They both agreed to give Costelloe's a miss on Friday and meet again after Harry had moved the money.

Jack Miller looked at his bedside clock. Eight a.m. He lifted Inga's hand from his chest, climbed out of bed and crossed the room to his desk. He powered up his laptop, went on-line and entered the Citibank website. Entering his user name and password he waited as the screen displayed the account of Sam Smithberg, the name he'd used to open the New York account. It confirmed that one of the many transactions executed overnight had successfully transferred two million dollars into the account. He logged off and logged onto the account he'd set up at Bank of America. This one under the name of William Johnson . Once again the screen confirmed a two million transfer in. Rubbing his hands with glee, he left Inga asleep, made himself a quick coffee, checked that he had the Sam Smithberg and William Johnson identifications, dressed and left.

At nine a.m. he entered the Park Avenue and 53rd Street branch of Citibank, presented his identity, and transferred two million dollars from Sam Smithberg's account to his numbered Swiss account. He walked a few blocks to Bank of America and transferred the two million from William Johnson's LA account to his own numbered account in Zurich. That done, he popped into the nearest travel agent and booked himself on the next flight to Europe. He also bought a ticket to Las Vegas in the name of Harry Roberts.

By eleven a.m. he was back in his apartment, watching Inga step, dripping wet, out of the shower. He tore his clothes off, pushed her back inside, turned on the shower and closed his eyes as she directed the fine spray over his head, his chest, finally settling lower as he rose in anticipation.

Later he sat at his desk, pulled a manila envelope out of a drawer, put fifty-thousand dollars and the airline ticket to Vegas into it. Finally he wrote a note to Harry and dropped it in. He reckoned that Harry would be out of it till tomorrow. Strong stuff the Englishman used and the broad was well paid to ensure Harry got enough to keep him out of commission for a couple of days. *Strictly a loser*, mused Miller, without a single feeling of remorse.

A few hours later he sat in first class, sipping a glass of champagne, as he watched Long Island disappear below.

The taxi dropped Harry Roberts at 60th and First and he shoved some bills into the driver's hand and didn't wait for the change. Minutes later he stepped off the fourth floor elevator, walked to Miller's apartment and rang the doorbell.

A healthy looking twenty-something blonde opened the door. Said, in a sultry German accent, "Jack is not here."

"Where is he?"

Roberts didn't wait for an answer, just went past her into the living room.

"What's your name?"

"Inga."

He wasn't really interested. He didn't want to swap bios, war stories, or bodily fluids with her.

But she persisted.

"I had nowhere to stay. Jack let me stay here. As long as I need, he said. Jack is very kind. Are you a friend of Jack? Are you Harry?"

"Yeah, I'm Harry."

"Jack left something for you. He said to make sure I gave it to you if you showed up."

She walked over to the bookcase, reached between the books, retrieved a large manila envelope and gave it to Harry.

"Can I get you a drink?"

"Good idea. Chivas. On the rocks."

One in the afternoon was earlier than usual for him. But what the hell. This was not a usual day. As she fixed his drink, he opened the envelope and a package of money slid into his lap. He slit the binder and counted fifty-thousand dollars. He reached inside and found an airline ticket to Las Vegas, a reservation at Caesar's Palace, and a note from Jack:

Jesus, Harry, couldn't find you anywhere. Did you shack up with that broad? Deal executed perfectly! Small change of plan. Figured we must celebrate. Meet me in Vegas. Then you can pick up your stuff in LA and live happily ever after! Jack.

No ID for the account. He'd expected Jack to have that ready to go, as promised. He picked up the phone and called Jack's cell. No answer. He tried again. No answer, just Jack's voice inviting the caller to leave a message. Harry didn't bother.

Guess he's saving it for Vegas, he reckoned. The flight was due to leave at five o'clock, in four hours' time. Harry downed the Chivas, abandoned Inga, and caught another taxi on First Avenue, telling the driver to take him to Tribeca. When he got there, he asked the taxi driver to wait for him, bounded into his apartment, located his own passport and packed a case with his best jacket and pants, his cool Jack Murphy shoes, said goodbye to the place, and minutes later sat in the taxi on his way to the airport.

One-arm bandits stood at attention at McCarron airport. Official greeters, Las Vegas style. But Roberts'd been here before, so no surprise.

The cabby boasted that he was a blackjack dealer by night and a cabby by day. Another story of the illusory dream. He dropped him at Caesars and Harry tipped him well.

They were expecting him this time. The computer screen, at the registration desk, flashed 'VIP'. In other words: big gambler, treat well. Jack had sure loaded the dice for him. It was obvious. The clerk's look of indifference suddenly changed to a huge smile of welcome. A young man rushed to get his bags and take him to his room.

His room! Take that back! More like a suite in Caesar's ancient Rome. It was in the Fantasy Tower. Circular Jacuzzi bathtub in the center of the bedroom. Huge circular bed, surrounded by a floor to ceiling diaphanous screen. A large circular mirror on the ceiling reflected the bed.

Roberts thought that it didn't get any better than this. He was wrong. It did.

Better came by the name of Maria. Exotic. Spanish blood, maybe.

"They told me to take care of you," she said, as she started to run a bath for him, "You must be tired from your journey. A bath and a massage is just what you need."

She stayed to watch him undress.

The Jacuzzi bubbled gently as he eased himself in, sat back, stretched his toes out to feel the jets, and looked up at Maria. She was undressing. Slowly. Just for his benefit.

Maria stepped into the jacuzzi and eased her body between his legs. In moments a young female attendant appeared with a bottle of Montrachet in a silver ice bucket. She poured two glasses, and then left the room.

Soon he felt very tired, unable to keep his eyes open. He could see Maria through a haze but he had a sense that the lights were going out and the room was turning dark, dark as midnight. Panic forced its way into his remaining consciousness and his heart began to race. He tried to get up but his legs wouldn't cooperate. He imagined that he could see Maria, standing back with a smile on her face. Somehow, with a superhuman effort, he managed to heave himself over the edge of the Jacuzzi.

As he hit the floor all the lights went out, and before he slid into darkness, his brain screamed one word in agony: *screwed!*

"Life isn't about finding yourself.
Life is about creating yourself."

George Bernard Shaw

Images of a life

Sweeney sat up and listened. Nothing. Only the silence. Deafening silence. Imaginings, he told himself, and snuggled back under the duvet. Just then he heard it again. *I didn't imagine it*, he almost shouted. He slid out from under the duvet. And listened. Nothing. Only the silence.

Tap...tap...tap

There, that's it. There it is again!

Tap...tap...tap

Like someone knocking on the door. But it's inside, not outside. Nothing now, silence again. *I'm not imagining this,* he told himself. *Am I going crazy,* he asked himself. No, no, no! He could feel, almost hear, the thumping of his heart. The pulse at his temple throbbed. Adrenalin. Pumping him up. Getting him ready to fight or flee. How do you fight a ghost?

Tap...tap...tap

He untangled himself from the duvet, swung his legs over the side of the bed, and struggled to get up. He reached for the bedside lamp, missed it and knocked it onto the floor. Unsteady, he felt has way around the bed and inched towards the door. Reaching it, he felt for the doorknob, turned it and pulled the door open. He walked out onto the landing and found the large flashlight he always left there for an emergency. An emergency that never happened.

Until now, he thought. He realized that he had no weapon. He stood quietly and listened. Silence. Maybe I really did imagine it, he thought. But no, no. That can't be. It was so real. He knew he had a large steel garden rake at the bottom of the stairs. At least he'd defend himself with that. So, with one hand against the wall, he steadied himself and slowly edged towards the stairs. At the top, he stood and listened again. Nothing.

The stairs were unlit but he decided to take them, one step at a time. Holding the handrail, he started. But he was halfway down when he lost his balance. He tried furiously to grab at something, to find the handrail again, to stop his fall. But that only launched him out and over. He could feel his total loss of control, could sense himself upside down and knew that he would hit the ground. He tried to turn his body to force a landing on his back. But failed. He hit the ground head first and immediately lost consciousness.

One week later

I remember ! I remember! What am I doing here? I'm in a coal-shed and I know that I am only eight or nine, maybe ten. *I do remember.* I am here to see the devil; actually tree branches projected through the keyhole onto the back wall. Images that moved in a very supernatural way. Could only be the devil ! I ran out of there, back to the classroom, to the desks with the ink-wells and the tall pens with the metal nibs. *I do remember!* In an act of mischief, I held out the pen and called the boy seated next to me. He turned and the nib stabbed him in the cheek. I could see the ink in the wound with the blood oozing out. *I know that the devil made me do it.*

And later that same day I could feel the pain in my legs from the lashes of the rod wielded by my father. I had drawn a stick figure of myself peeing. It seemed perfectly natural and innocent to me. But he made it dirty. *I know that the devil made him do it.*

Why do I remember these things, I ask myself. I have no control over this. My mind keeps digging them up. Now I am twelve years old and I am attending Mass in the chapel at my college. I am returning to my seat and I can't stop coughing. I spit the communion out of my mouth and it flies through the air and lands on the seat of the pew in front of me. I am terrified. I don't know what to do. I've been told that the communion, the eucharist, could only be touched by the sacred, consecrated hands of the priest. But I have no option. I pick the communion off the seat with my hand and put it back on my tongue. *I know that the devil made me do this.*

I remember the wakes : summer after summer, coming home from College to find another body laid out ....always at home in Ireland. Kneeling by my grandfather's body in his bed, listening to the chant and drone of the rosary, being forced to touch his cold, cold hands, thinking that he might unclasp them and grab me. A house filled with mourners who laughed and talked, injecting the wake with humour and pathos. Telling stories about the departed and stories that must surely be untrue, or exaggerations at least; a woman who had suffered from scoliosis. curvature of the spine, who'd been tied down in the bed to keep her straight. Then someone cuts the bindings and she springs 'to life' and people flee, tripping over each other as they try to jump the 'half-door'. *Surely the devil made them do it.*

Where am I? I don't know. I must still be in bed. And still asleep. Dreaming. Imagining. I toss and turn in my head. But I don't feel my body tossing and turning.

Where am I? I know that I am afraid. And cold, inside and outside. I am standing in the jinks, the boys' toilet at College. A place of very dark slate and very little light, each urinal separated by high slate. A large square place. Used as the venue for duels. It's a dark evening and showery too. I am standing beside many other students who are there for the fight. There's a hush as the two fighters enter the 'ring', a theatre in the round, in the centre of the audience. I recognize one of the fighters, Jesse James. John Kelly, but we always knew him as Jesse James. Jesse was our hero. He stood up for us. He fought the system for us. The fight is brutal. We are buffeted back and forth as the fighters bounce off us, as they would have off a rope in a boxing ring. Somehow I know I am not here. Yet I know that I must be. It is very real. Soon it is over. The loser lies on the ground, bruised and bloody. Jesse is the winner. *I don't believe the devil made them do it. The devil would not have let Jesse win.*

Yes, I remember Jesse. I am sitting at my desk in the lonely study hall, imprisoned there every evening. But this evening is different. The President enters, accompanied by Jesse. He takes the stage and makes a speech about the expected punishment for breaking the rules.

We know that Jesse is going to pay that punishment for all of us. The President cites Jesse's list of violations and states clearly the punishment to be meted out for every one. He instructs Jesse to face him and hold out his hand. Jesse, proud and erect, shoulders back, faces the President and holds out his right hand. The President produces his long leather strap and swings it high and back over his shoulder, bringing it down on Jesse's right hand. Jesse takes it. Does not flinch. The President continues. But Jesse still stands tall. Then the President instructs Jesse to hold out his left hand. I can see that the President is tired now but he swings that strap high and back to get the most leverage. Again and again on Jesse's left hand. We can see that Jesse is in a lot of pain. But we can also see that Jesse is never going to plead for forgiveness, never going to admit defeat. At the end, it is obvious that the President has left the study hall, a defeated man. *I know that the devil must have made him do it.*

I do indeed remember. But is this memory real? Or is it imagined? It looks like the college chapel has been turned into a courtroom. Isn't that some kind of a sacrilege? The chapel is filled with all final year students. I am sitting in the front row. I know that that is not by choice. I'd never want to be in the front row. The altar has been turned into a dais. All the eccentric professors and the President too, are seated there: Sam, Flah, The Bird, Wee Rusty, Coof, Quick

Draw McGraw, Wee Alfie, The Goat, Tooly Wooly. A sense of doom pervades. We are expecting to get our finals. Expecting to graduate. But we know that we will fail. And that some terrible injustice is about to be done. *And we know that the devil is behind it all.*

Three weeks later

Doctor Hooke entered the intensive care unit and examined Sweeney. No change. Now in the fourth week of a coma. He gave him a thorough examination. Tested his reflex to pain. Tested for reflexive eye movements and any change in pupil size. He spoke very loudly to him and looked for any kind of arousal: noises from his voice or any movement. He even squirted ice-cold water into his ear canals to see if he can get any eye reactions. Nothing. No reaction at all.

Four weeks later

I am in a parallel universe. I must be. I've always known that the past, the present, and the future all live together. And now the past is invading my present. I am cold. And very afraid. I am standing, spread-eagled against a wall, guns pointed at my back. The clothing patterns that I had so carefully packed now lay scattered at my feet. This was the special police force known as the 'B Specials', a force known for a disregard of the law and a penchant for the use of force. Force driven by reaction, by racism, by fear. I'd already answered all their questions after they blocked the road and removed me from my Lambretta scooter. I told them that the neatly tied packages in strong brown paper that hung from my handlebars were cloth pattern that I was taking to

The Royal Showband to help them select a new outfit for their band. But they didn't believe me. Or they didn't care. So they ripped my packages open and threw the pattern books on the ground. And then they laughed at me. Finally they lost interest in me. They told me to move on but didn't help me to gather up my pattern books. I scrambled to gather them up, tie some cord around them, kick start the scooter, and move away. Still afraid, I waited for the bullet in my back.

Why am I feeling sick? The floor is rolling. I am on a boat. I am suffocating from smoke. Smoke from cigarettes and pipes. Almost a dense cloud. I must get air. I stumble across the room to a stairway. It is dark. I put my foot on the bottom step and try to take one step at a time. But I can feel myself losing my balance and slipping. I fall down and hit my head. I don't know how long I have lain here but the smoke is making me feel nauseous. My head hurts. I struggle back onto the stairs and, once more, step by step I make it up to the top deck. The sea is rough and the boat is rolling back and forth. People are sitting on benches, drinking pints and smoking. But the sea air is blowing it away. I learn that I am on the Irish Sea on a crossing to England. I've never been to England before. I wonder what awaits me.

I can't breathe. I am climbing and climbing. Where am I now? I do remember. I'm in Canada. Crossed the Atlantic on a boat from Liverpool. I'm in Quebec. Outside Quebec City. I am doing one of those things I've always wanted to do. Climb up to the Plains of Abraham. I know that I am somewhere on the 398 steps on the stairway to the Plains, where the Irish

General Wolfe defeated the French General Montcalm. Wolfe's win led to the French conceding Canada to the British. But I am exhausted. I must rest now. I sit down and I can feel myself falling asleep. But I must stay awake. I must reach the Plains. I have come this far. I can not give up now. I must stay awake.

Where am I? I'm wearing an army uniform and carrying a rifle. I'm in a deep trench as I clasp a hand grenade close to my chest, pull the pin, throw it over the trench, duck down and wait for the boom. Other soldiers wait in the trench with me. One tells me that we are on the infiltration course and that we have to do it now, in the daytime, and again in the dark, at night-time. Soon we get the command to move out. I climb out of the trench and lie flat on my back, using my rifle to prop up the barbed wire so that I can slide my way through. Crawling in the open I pass bunkers lined with sand bags. Explosions rock the bunkers. Red tracer bullets streak the sky above my head. Very soon I hit the barbed wire again. On my back with my rifle across my chest I slide under the barbed wire. But suddenly I am no longer there. *Where am I? I don't know. This must be a dream. I've always had the strangest and most exciting dreams.*

Where am I now? I don't know. I am lost. I am not anywhere. My head hurts. Why does my head hurt so much? Did I get hurt? I don't remember. I don't remember anything. I think I'll just go back to sleep again.

Two months later

They raised the wicker coffin holding Sweeney's body. Holding steady, they balanced him as they turned to pass the people acting as a vanguard on the stairs. No voices, no prayers, only silence. On the ground floor, they stopped and rested him. Others had assembled on the street outside. Almost in anticipation, the people fell into an orderly cortege. They raised him again and took the lead. Twenty minutes later, they arrived at the entrance to Mount Jerome crematorium. A simple humanist service followed in the chapel. No one came to collect his ashes.

A cold chill in January

You always wondered

You know there was no-one in the bedroom when you felt your way in the darkness to the toilet. They say there's a cold feeling in the air when there's another presence in the room but you convinced yourself that it was natural to feel a cold chill in January.

She didn't stir on her side of the bed. You always woke up quietly. You always slid your feet out onto the cold floor and eased the rest of your body out without tugging the bedclothes. She never knew that you went to the toilet three times during the night. You never told her. You didn't want her to know that your body was beginning to show the signs of wear.

You never flushed the toilet at night. The filling tank made too much noise. It would surely wake her up. She always left her watch on the glass shelf by the sink. That's the only way you knew the time. But you really didn't want to know the time. You always left your own watch on the side table by your bed, in the dark where you couldn't read it till daybreak.

You groped behind you with your right hand and found the hot water bottle that she had put in your side of the bed. It was tepid now at three in the morning. You slid under the duvet and pulled it up so that your head was covered, just enough to hide you but not enough to suffocate you. You turned over on your left side so that your good left ear was silenced by the pillow. Your deaf right ear didn't matter.

You lay there as you did every night, trying to get back to sleep. Eventually you did return to sleep but never to the dream you were in before you woke up.

She was always awake before you. You would

wake up to the feeling of her arm around your waist, her loins warm against the small of your back and her lips brushing the nape of your neck. You always turned over and blessed your good fortune as your arms encircled her body and you kissed her gently on her eyelids, the tip of her nose, and her soft inviting lips.

You always wondered what she would do that morning when you didn't respond. That morning you were certain would come when she would wake up, stretch and turn around to encircle your waist and brush her lips against your cold, cold neck. That morning when you wouldn't turn over to hold her. That last morning of your life. You always wondered about that.

You were still wondering when you realized you were awake. It was morning and the light was filtering into the bedroom. You had wakened by yourself this morning. You turned and looked over. She was still asleep. You felt as though you had been given a gift today. The gift of morning that she always brought to you. You would bring it to her.

You turned over and circled her waist with your arm. You brushed your lips against her cold, cold neck.

"Vengeance is mine. Good enough for the Lord, good enough for me"

The Avenger

The two boys, breathless, reached the west corner of the big study hall and flattened themselves against the granite wall. Night had fallen and the wind had reached gale force. Sleety rain sliced the air like sheets of broken glass. The trees bent and groaned. Wearing short trousers, their legs were scorched red from knees to ankles.

They could see the flashlight coming towards them and they knew they'd have to run again. So they left the shelter of the wall and dashed past the handball court as the lightning illuminated everything. Exposed, they cut across the front lawn and ran towards the outer wall. They could hear the loud squelch of running feet behind them.

A line of ancient oak trees stood like sentries inside the outer wall. They hid between the trees, hoping their pursuers would pass them by. But that was a false hope. The flashlight reached the trees, weaving in and out, getting closer and closer. Panicked, Patrick, the older boy, started to climb the nearest tree. Terry, the younger boy, tried to follow but couldn't. So he ran, blindly, out of the shelter of the trees. Patrick sat on a branch as the flashlight passed beneath him. He had stopped breathing and his heart thumped so loudly he imagined they must hear it. But they moved on, following Terry as he fled.

Now alone and terrified, Terry ran into the blinding rain, his lungs seared from the effort. Lightning flashed again, silhouetting the old ruined tower that stood inside the north-east boundary of the school. He stumbled over the uneven lumpy ground and, as the lightning flashed again, he saw the scaffolding clinging to the side of the tower. Erected recently by workmen hired to halt the deterioration, it seemed to offer him hope. Reaching the bottom of the scaffolding, he saw a wooden ladder the workmen used to get up to the first level. He started to climb as the lightning ended and the tower once again became pitch-black like the night above. On the first level he crawled over the rough wooden planks that bridged the gap between the metal scaffolding rods until he could feel the tower wall. Standing up he grabbed the next horizontal rod and, bracing himself between it and the wall, leveraged himself to the top level. Now he could hear voices nearby and streaks of light from a flashlight threw ribbons of white across the scaffolding. Trapped now, he realized he had nowhere to go. If he went back down he knew they'd get him. Backing up he found himself on a ledge near the door. He squeezed into the door frame, hoping to somehow disappear.

"We've got him! He's in the tower!" The first priest with the flashlight looked back at his companion, triumph in his voice.

"There he is!" he cried, shining his flashlight upwards until the boy stood transfixed in the glare, like a rabbit caught in a car's headlights.

"Don't! Take the light off his eyes!" The second priest, cautious, held the first priest's arm, "Let me talk to him."

The first priest hesitated and then moved the light away from the boy's face, "All right, we'll try it your way."

"Terry, can you hear me?

No answer.

The boy stood, fixed like a gargoyle, urine dripping down his bare legs and running into his socks.

"Terry, we are not going to hurt you. We only want you to give us your camera phone. The one you took the photos with."

No answer.

"Terry, you know we can't let you keep the photos, don't you?"

No answer.

"Terry, give us the phone and we'll say no more about it. Don't you want to go back to your room? You could catch your death out here on a night like this. You don't want to die over a few photos, do you Terry?"

No answer.

The first priest, '*I told you so*' in his tone of voice, cut in, "OK, we tried it your way. It didn't work, did it? Now we'll do it my way."

With the flashlight carving a path ahead of him, he moved to the foot of the ladder and started to climb. The boy saw him coming but he was cornered, nowhere to go. The priest, agile and sure footed, soon reached the top level of scaffolding, within easy reach of the boy.

"Give it to me! Now!"

The boy squeezed even further into the door opening. Sobs gurgled somewhere deep in his throat.

The priest, patience exhausted, reached for the boy. But the boy, terrified, tried to squeeze further into the door, lost his balance and fell. Seconds later, they heard the thump of his body on the rocks below.

"Oh, dear God, he's dead!" The words, almost a wail, escaped from the second priest as they stood over the boy's body.

The first priest took the boy's pulse and said, "Yes, he's dead." He knelt down beside the boy and searched the pockets of his school blazer. Then he searched the pockets of his trousers.

"Nothing!"

"Maybe he lost it somewhere tonight. Or maybe it's lying around here. Could have fallen out of his pocket."

They started to search, lighting arcs around the body, guessing how far away from the tower a phone could have landed. After fifteen minutes they abandoned the search.

"What will we do about him?" asked the second priest.

"Nothing! Leave him here! When he's missing tomorrow, the prefects will search for him. Someone will find him."

"There'll be an investigation."

"No, there will be no investigation. It's an accident. Another dare gone wrong. Climbing the tower on a stormy night."

The second priest couldn't disagree. He knew that some of the boys got up to daredevil antics, climbing the walls after lights out, things like that. But Terry was never one of them.

"What will we do about the phone? What if it's lost and somebody finds it?"

"I don't think he lost the phone. He hid it. Or he gave it to someone."

They had almost reached the priests' residence hall and the storm had abated. The first priest stopped, turned to the second and said, with conviction: "That's it! He gave the phone to someone. We followed two of them tonight. And we lost one of them. Who was he?"

"We don't know."

"Well, who was young Terry friendly with? Who was he close to? "

"That's it, he wasn't close to anyone. He was quiet. A loner. Kept to himself. I tried to get him to participate. But he always held back, stayed on the fringes."

"Well, he must have a friend somewhere. He wasn't alone out there tonight. We've got to find that other boy. Soon!"

Monsignor Thomas Fallon, President Emeritus of St. Curnan's, still retained an office and a position as faculty advisor at the school. Now seventy-three, his power and influence remained undiminished. A lesser man would have been moved to one of the Church's retirement homes to spend the rest of his days in anonymity. But not Monsignor Fallon, who was politically connected all the way to the College of Cardinals in Rome. Plump and effete in manner, he sat in utter disbelief as Father Roland Cormack finished talking.

"Roland, this is a disaster!"

"I know! I wish I could turn the clock back."

"They'll say that you killed this boy!"

"But I didn't. He fell. It was an accident."

"Listen to yourself. If it's discovered that you followed this boy up into that tower and caused his death, they'll charge you. Murder or manslaughter, what's the difference? It'll be a show trial. They're out to get us now. Here, in the US, everywhere! This is a disaster!"

"No, no! There's nothing to suggest I was there when the boy fell. Only Father Nugent knows. And he won't say anything."

"How can you be so sure?"

"He's a wimp! You know him. He wouldn't say 'boo to a fly'."

"And why was he out there with you if he's such a wimp?"

"He knew about the photos. He thought he could talk to Terry. Get the phone from him. He liked the boy and he wanted to protect him."

"Father Nugent knows too much, that's what I think. And I think he's a risk."

"No, our big risk is that phone. The photos. We don't know what Terry Joyce did with it, or who he might have given it to."

"It's *your* big risk, not *our* big risk. Find that phone. Search everywhere. Find the boy who was with him last night."

"And if I don't find the phone?"

"Well, then you'd better hope it's lost, buried somewhere forever!"

After Father Cormack had left, Monsignor Fallon sat for a long time in contemplation. Then he picked up the phone and called Rome.

Next day Roland Cormack departed Dublin Airport on *Alitalia Flight AZ 3581*_at 2:15 pm. With a stopover in Paris, he arrived at Leonardo Da Vinci Airport in Rome at 9 pm, fifteen minutes late. Craving privacy, he avoided the express train and took one of the white cabs instead. Cardinal Volpe was expecting him at the Vatican

Even at sixty, Father Bernard Flaherty, the Irish teacher, was athletic and virile with the body of a man twenty years younger. While others read their morning breviary in their rooms, he donned a pair of sneakers and read his as he fast walked around the perimeter of the college grounds.

The light morning mist began to lift as he reached the stand of oak trees. He lifted his head to enjoy the beginning of a new day. But the sight ahead brought him to a sudden stop.

He stood, transfixed, clenching his breviary until his knuckles started to hurt. Shaking himself, he took the final few steps until he stood directly under the body that hung from the tree: a boy in the school blazer, short grey trousers, socks, no shoes. His neck twisted grotesquely out of the make-shift noose and his swollen tongue protruded from hismouth, gobs of saliva and mucous forming a trail down the front of his blazer.

Father Flaherty blessed himself and sank to his knees. He couldn't reach the boy so he recited the Act of Contrition where he knelt and asked God for forgiveness.

Then he got up, turned and ran towards the College.

He bounded through the front door, almost colliding with a group of students emerging from their breakfast in the refectory. He took the stairs two at a time, catching President McCafferty as he was about to enter his office. Sliding to a halt, he startled the President who turned around to see a red-faced Father Flaherty gasping for breath with sweat trickling down his cheeks.

"Father, what's wrong?"

"It's terrible, the boy ... he's dead!"

"Come in, come in ..." President McCafferty, now alarmed, gripped Father Flaherty by the arm, pulled him inside the office, and closed the door.

"What're you talking about? Who's dead?"

"Patrick Carty. He's hanging – from that tree – look out your window!"

Father Flaherty had gained control again. His face was still red but now from anger. He steered the President to the large office window the overlooked the front portico and commanded a view of the lawns that swept down to the main gate and the line of oak trees, now majestic in the morning sun.

"He's hanging from that tree! And we're responsible. We took that boy's life."

President McCafferty stood transfixed before the window. He couldn't see the boy. His eyes were blurry with emotion. Somewhere deep inside he managed to get a grip on himself and turned to face Father Flaherty.

"Bernard, I'm as shocked as you. But I reject your accusation that we're to blame." With that, he strode to his desk, sat down and pulled the phone towards him.

But Father Bernard Flaherty would not be dissuaded, "I warned you! I knew this would happen. First that Joyce boy, now young Carty. Somebody has to pay. We have to take responsibility for this!"

"Bernard, Bernard, I've listened to you rant and rave like this so many times. You've alienated most of our faculty with your wild accusations."

"Wild accusations! Have you not been reading the newspapers? People have spat on me as I walked down the street. Spat on me! Do you hear me? Me, a priest, and they spat on me! I warned all of you that we must do something about this. Now it's too late!"

"Father Bernard, you're not helping. I do not want you charging around the school like this. Go to your room and pray for the soul of this unfortunate boy. I'm going to call the Gardai now. Then I'm going to call an assembly. I want the faculty and the students to hear this news from me. And I want the impact contained. Contained! Do you understand?"

But Father Bernard Flaherty was already on his way out, banging the large oak door behind him as he left.

A different Father Bernard Flaherty emerged from President McCafferty's office. He was no longer the light-hearted person who'd been out for his morning run. With the loose easy-going stride gone, the body had stiffened, the arms swung threateningly, the gait now one of an automaton, even the open face now closed into a bleak impenetrable visage. His hair, naturally tousled, sleeked back with sweat, now seemed designed for more serious purpose.

Once inside his own room, he put down his breviary and went to his bureau, pulled out the top drawer, retrieved a bottle of pills prescribed to him and clearly marked *prozac.* He opened the bottle and tipped one into the palm of his hand. Then he reached into the drawer again and squeezed two paracetamol tablets from a sheet of tinfoil. At the sink, he filled a glass with water and washed all three down his throat.

He sat down on the floor, in the lotus position, and started to chant in Latin ...

At exactly twelve noon Father Bernard Flaherty stepped onto the handball court. A tall three-sided concrete built court, it served as a whipping boy for him. On evenings and weekends, when he wasn't jogging, he was on the court, usually with an attentive, hypnotized audience. Boys would silently line both sides of the court, hands in pockets, watching every move he made, every time his hand whacked the ball with definite malice up against that wall. Every time he hit the ball, the boys' hands would strike in unison, punching inside the pockets of their trousers. This action was called *hinching*. Seemingly unaware of their involuntary complicity they would stand transfixed until he finished, *hinching* every time he struck the ball. But today he had no audience. He held the ball firmly in his hand, bounced it off the ground, and struck it hard with his right hand.

He kept this up until he collapsed, red-faced and breathless.

His foot slipped but he hung on. Suspended twenty feet above the ground, he hung on to a small tree that grew stubbornly out of the rock fissure. Winded, with muscles that hurt, sheer willpower and revenge drove him on. Finding sounder footing, he rested and looked around.

Everything looked ghostly in the dusk. The lights of the town glimmered in the distance. Looking up, he could see the top of the college walls five or six feet above his head. He started to climb again.

Almost there.

The luminous dial of his watch read 10 pm. Stars decorated the sky above. He sat in a sheltered cove behind the wall. He'd been here for over an hour. When he reached here, there'd been enough light left to show the hundreds of cigarette butts that now carpeted the ground beneath his feet. Students' secret smoke hole. Well hidden but holding a good view of the college and its grounds, perfect for keeping a look-out for the prefects or even the Dean.

Clothed totally in black, he wore a black ski cap that could easily convert to a balaclava. A rope hung, lariat style, over his left shoulder.

It's time, he said to himself.

The school grounds were deserted. All the students were now in their dorm rooms, in bed with the lights out. Four or five windows shone like beacons on the second floor of the faculty residence hall. One light shone out of the large French windows overlooking the roof of the main building's entrance porch. The President's office.

Rested after his climb, he ran across the sloping front lawn until he reached the shelter of the main building. Out of breath, he stopped for a minute and then moved cautiously, close to the building, until he reached the entrance porch.

Taking the rope from his shoulder, he threw it up and lassoed one of the marble stanchions mounted on top of the porch. He hooked the end to his belt and rappelled himself to the roof of the porch. Light from the French windows suffused out in a circle, leaving the edges of the porch in darkness. He looped the rope around the stanchion and, carrying one end, crawled across the porch to the edge of the French doors. Slightly ajar to let in some fresh air, he could see President McCafferty sitting erect at his desk, reading from a stack of papers. In his late sixties, his bald held alleviated by clumps of white hair at his temples, his ruddy face testimony to the outdoor athletic life he had led as a young man, as a star of the local Gaelic football club, he seemed preoccupied and totally unaware that he was about to have a visitor.

Vengeance is mine. Good enough for the Lord, good enough for me.

President Sam McCafferty dropped his papers and stood up in shock. The black clad man had entered his office through the French windows and was now standing holding the end of a rope. He said nothing, just stood there, fully intent on unnerving him. President McCafferty thought fast. Too late to call anyone to help. Besides they didn't live in a high risk place so they had never felt the need for their own security force. *No, I'm on my own, he thought, I'll have to talk my way through this.*

"Who are you?"

No answer.

"What do you want?"

No answer.

"I have no money or valuables here. If you've come to rob me, you've wasted your time."

No answer.

"If you talk to me, maybe I can help you."

No answer. The man took a couple of steps into the office and looked around, as though searching for something.

"Won't you tell me what you want? Maybe I can help you."

No answer.

President McCafferty realized he was getting nowhere and wondered if he could make a run for it. If he could move out from behind his desk and edge his way towards the door, maybe he could do it. So he came out from behind his desk and stood to the side, saying,

"If you're in some kind of trouble, maybe I can help you. You can talk to me."

No answer.

The man's eyes seemed angry. The rest of his face was covered in a black balaclava.

"I won't tell anybody. No need to involve the police. Whatever trouble you're in, you need to talk to someone."

No answer.

The President decided to take the first step towards the door. But, as he did so, the man took some things out of his pocket and threw them at him. They hit his chest and dropped on the floor at his feet.

"Pick them up!"

The voice, loud and angry, showed no sign of weakness. The President found himself thrown off-balance, his plan of escape unattainable. Nothing to do but obey, play this thing out, and hope for the best.

He bent down and picked up the items from the floor. Students' caps with the school emblems pinned on the front.

"Look inside. Read the names!"

President McCafferty read the names and his ruddy face suddenly lost all its colour. Now he knew the visitor's purpose. His legs started to tremble,

Fuelled by fear, the President made a dash for the door. Too late. The man rushed him, grabbed his soutane so fiercely that it ripped from the neck to the waist. The President had never been a fighter and had lived a life of non-violence, but now he kicked out at his assailant and landed a blow to the man's thigh. Which only infuriated the man who swung his fist and connected with the President's jaw, stunning him and knocking him to the ground. Vulnerable now, the President could feel the rope around his neck and hear the man's voice, a voice vaguely familiar.

"An eye for an eye. A tooth for a tooth. Isn't that what the bible says? Well, isn't it? A life for a life!"

The man tightened the noose around the President's neck and, with almost superhuman strength, began to drag him across the floor towards the French windows. The President tried to dig his heels in, tried to resist, but the man tightened the noose. Once out through the French windows, the man grabbed the other end of the rope, already looped around the stanchion, and commenced to tug, just like a tug-of-war game. The President, unable to resist, slid inexorably towards the edge of the roof. Finally the man kicked him over the edge and braced himself as the President's body jerked the rope taut.

Vengeance is mine. Good enough for the Lord, good enough for me.

An angry Monsignor Thomas Fallon bounded down the stairs of St. Curnan's, rushed out the front door, and headed for his car. In twenty minutes he was on the main road heading west. Checked the clock on the dashboard: almost four thirty. He turned on the radio. Music wasn't his thing, certainly not the pop tunes that filled the airwaves from Radio2. Then he realized that *The Last Word* talk-show was about to start on TodayFM. *That'll do nicely,* he thought, *help to kill the next hour or so.* Leaning over to turn on the radio, the car behind annoyed him. Even though it wasn't dark, its headlights were on full. Maybe he'll turn off and I'll lose him soon. Cautioning himself to relax, he turned up the volume and drove at a steady sixty miles an hour.

The Avenger had been waiting for this opportunity for days. The monsignor was evil. He knew that. And no-one had done anything about it. Now the monsignor had covered up a crime and moved the guilty one out of the country. Moved him to Rome where he'd get protection. The Church had failed. Failed to purge itself of this evil. The Church had lost its way. These evil people were no better than the Templars who used to reject Christ and_spit on the cross. But God found a way to make them pay. We burned them at the stake. Well, I am doing God's work. I will make these evil ones pay. An eye for an eye, a tooth for a tooth. He pressed down on the accelerator and closed the gap between his own car and the monsignor's. Let him experience fear. Yes, that's what I intend for the monsignor. Fear!

Monsignor Fallon almost swore out loud. If he'd been accustomed to using swear words when angry, he'd have done so. He pounded the steering wheel and screamed: *damn! damn! damn!.* The high beams penetrated his car, reflecting off his mirrors and distracting him. He was annoyed. Why would someone follow him? He had no enemies. And he had no money. They'd get nothing if they robbed him. Maybe I can lose him, he thought. He pushed down on the accelerator and watched the needle move from sixty to sixty-five to seventy. He didn't feel safe at this speed, especially now that it was dark, but he had to try and get away. It had started to rain and his windscreen fogged up. He strained to see as the high beams behind continued to drill into him. Maybe I should get off the road, he thought. The village of Cong lay a mile ahead and he decided to stop and seek refuge there.

Losing his concentration, he suddenly realized that the speedometer needle was nudging seventy-five as he entered the village of Cong. He hit the brakes and tried to slow down. But the rain had slicked the ground and he missed his turn-off into the main street of the village. The car spun out of control, almost hitting the dark limestone plinth of the Market Cross, and crossed the street at an angle narrowly missing the corner houses on each side until it finally slid into the old wall surrounding Cong Abbey. Steam rose out of the radiator and the bonnet had crumpled like a piece of cheap tin. The adrenalin was telling him to flee and the seat belts were cutting into his neck and shoulder telling him not to move. He released the seat belt and looked over his shoulder to see the street in darkness behind him. No sign of the car that had followed him. Maybe this is God's will that I should come to the Abbey on a night like this. Fumbling under the seat, he found a flashlight he'd stowed there. Hoping that the batteries still worked, he turned it on. It shone but dimly. The batteries were on their last legs. It wouldn't last long. The rain had eased off and he made a decision. He'd visit the Abbey and pray. Then he'd find somewhere to stay for the night and get a garage to take care of his car in the morning.

Pulling the hood of his raincoat over his head, he had enough street light to let him see the entrance to the abbey, a few yards ahead. Founded by the last High King of Ireland, Turlough O'Conor, in the early twelfth century for the Augustinians, its ruined walls still stood, a monument to its grandeur. Passing through its very beautiful doorway, he turned the flashlight on and briefly illuminated the intricate carvings that framed it. Even though he'd been there many times before, he was still in awe of the artistry.

He stepped through the doorway and stood inside the great abbey church. The rain had stopped and the sky now served as a huge vaulted roof. He felt the majesty of God here and, using the flashlight, stepped over the tombstones that paved the floor until he reached the centre. Kneeling then, he clasped his hands in silent prayer.

The sound of footsteps on gravel brought him out of his reverie of prayer in time to see the rays of a very powerful flashlight streak across the walls at the gable end. Painfully, he forced his arthritic hips to support his legs as he stood. But the flashlight, almost a searchlight had now found him and he stood there in its glow.

"Monsignor, so good of you to wait for me." The voice was strong, even theatrical, with a strong sense of threat.

"Who are you? What do you want with me?"

"It doesn't matter who I am. It's God who wants you, wants a reckoning with you."

That was enough for the Monsignor. This man sounded deranged. He'd have to get away from him. So he turned and ran, stumbling over the large flat tombstones. If he could make it to the forest at the end of the open cloisters, he might be able to hide. He knew the direction but he couldn't see and his flashlight was almost dead. But he could see more from the powerful light that his pursuer splayed back and forth. He dashed ahead, then tripped and fell, the flashlight clattering away from him. Hurting badly, he got up again and finally made it though the church wall into the cloisters at the rear. He knew that if he followed the path straight ahead, it would lead him into the dense Ashford forest where he might be able to hide.

He could sense his pursuer closing in so he started to run, blindly, tripped and fell almost immediately. Stunned, he tried to get up but couldn't. Then he felt strong hands behind him, lifting him and holding him. He was powerless to fight back as he felt some kind of restraints tying his wrists together behind his back. His attacker said nothing. Monsignor Fallon fell back on the only defence he knew: prayer. He prayed as his attacker pulled and dragged him down the pathway between the trees until they reached the river. He couldn't see it clearly but he could hear the rush of its water.

The Avenger knew what he must do. But he wanted the monsignor to know why. He wanted to give him time to repent before he met his God. An old abandoned stone house, the walls still standing, stood out over the river. Used as a fish house by the friars, it was constructed over the river to trap the fish in a crib underneath. Swimming about they touched a wire that rang a bell to let the cook know. The Avenger thought that the old fish house would do nicely. Dragging the monsignor onto it, he looped a rope through the restraints on his wrist and pushed him over the edge until he was waist deep in the river. He tied the rope around a metal_barrier that had been installed to protect the tourists and stood up. The monsignor had said nothing, only prayed all the time, and now prayed even louder. He took the bible out of his pocket, held the flashlight over it, and in his deep theatrical voice, started to read:

"Monsignor, you must already know why you are here. You must know the crimes you have committed. No? You do not defend yourself. Yes, go on, pray. Maybe the Lord will forgive you. After all he is compassionate, we think."

"But I will read from the bible so you can listen to his anger"

In Jude 1:7, *the Lord says that "Sodom and Gomorrah and the surrounding towns gave themselves up to sexual immorality and perversion"*

Monsignor Fallon had stopped praying and was trying to speak. But only phlegm and grunts emitted from his mouth. He could not utter any words. His tongue failed him and he could feel his heart racing and then skipping and stopping and spluttering. He could hear his torturer's voice clearly and it seemed familiar to him. But he believed that he was only imagining that. He tried to speak again but his larynx had shut down.

"And, Monsignor, you and those like you are no better than the people of Sodom and Gomorrah! I see you trying to speak but the Lord won't let you defend yourself. No, there is no defence for you. You are guilty. And what punishment does the Lord dictate?"

"He says, *'If your right eye makes you do wrong, take it out and throw it away. It is better to lose a part of your body, than for your whole body to be thrown into hell. If your hand or your foot makes you do wrong, cut it off and throw it away! It is better for you to enter into life without hands or feet than to have two hands and two feet and be thrown into the fire that burns for ever.'* "

"And what does he tell us to do? You must know the answer."

"He tells us to *'take the man or woman who has done this evil deed to your city gate and stone that person to death'* "

"But I will leave you here like this and if the Lord has compassion he will save you!"

The water lapped over the monsignor's chest and he no longer felt anything in his legs. Before he lapsed into unconsciousness, something screamed in his brain "I know that voice! I know who he is."

The Avenger left Cong in a state of numbness. He did not feel any remorse. He never felt remorse. Driving with his right hand he fingered his rosary beads in his left. He wasn't saying the rosary. He mostly used the beads as a touchstone, a comforter, a device to control his emotions. He knew that he was God's instrument. God had asked him to clear out the temple, to pluck out the eyes that offended, to cut off the hands that scandalized. His work had only just begun. He inserted the CD of Biscantorat and hit the play button. Adjusting the volume, he almost closed his eyes as The Sound of The Spirit from Glenstal Abbey *filled the air*

The music soothed him and he began to relax. As the car warmed up, the tension and anger left his body and he could feel himself become Father Bernard Flaherty again.

The chapel appeared like a ship in the mist. A triangular shape, beached on the mountainy roadside, buffeted by the rain and wind, the invitation *Stop and Pray,* black on white, glared at Father Bernard Flaherty in the headlights of his car.

He pulled into the small empty parking place in front of the church. One light shone inside through the large transparent front windows. He sat for a while, then got out, pulled the hood of his coat over his head, and strode through the rain to the front door. It was open. He entered and looked around. Empty, as though it had been reserved especially for him. For a brief moment, he wondered if this church really existed, wondered if it would really be here if he drove past in tomorrow's daylight.

He walked slowly up the centre aisle until he reached the altar rail. Without hesitation, he knelt and let his wet raincoat drop to the ground at his feet, puddles of rainwater soon accumulating on the tiles that surrounded him.

And he prayed.

"Dear Lord, I did not ask for this. Just as you did not ask for the suffering you endured, for the brutal crucifixion, so I have not asked to be your instrument of vengeance. But your church on earth must be cleansed of its sins. Your people must see that the will of God is carried out. Your people will know the signs. They will know that these defilers have been punished by you. They will know the signs. Just as you prophesized against the Philistines when you promised that you would stretch out your hand against them, carry out great vengeance on them and punish them in your wrath. They knew that you were the Lord when you took vengeance on them."

Slowly he rose to his feet, raised the raincoat from the floor and pulled it around his shoulders. He genuflected, turned around and walked briskly out of the church. The rain had turned to a fine drizzle, peppering his face and filling him with renewed energy. He felt cleansed, refreshed, his soul blessed by God. He climbed into his car and headed towards Athlone. It was Easter holidays at St. Curnan's and he wasn't expected back for two weeks. Enough time to absorb the news about the monsignor.

He headed for the monastery in Mullingar. They were expecting him.

He would be able to find solace there.

And await the word of the Lord.

XANADU: North of the Great Wall, the Site of **Xanadu** encompasses the remains of Kublai Khan's legendary capital city, designed by the Mongol ruler's Chinese advisor Liu Bingzhdong in 1256. **Xanadu** is the name that's been used by parents who are considering unisex or non-gendered baby names.

XANADU

The DJ at Xanadu wore a red beehive hairdo, false eyelashes, press-on fingernails and a big, fluffy boa draped around her neck. 'She' had always fancied Larry Sanderson but he had never been interested. It was Saturday and she spotted him at the bar.

"Larry, Honey, where have you been lately?" she gushed.

"Working, Sydney. Just working. Nothing more exotic," said Larry.

"You know what they say about that, Honey. All work and no play makes Larry a dull boy. Just let me know when you want to play. I can promise you a good time."

"Sydney, love, thanks. I think I just want to be alone tonight."

"Honey, you don't know what you're missing," said Sydney in a huff as she glided back to play some more selections before the show began.

Xanadu was an upscale gay entertainment place with a bar, restaurant and club. Larry Sanderson seldom went there. It was a bit too yuppie for him. But he enjoyed the shows. Larry managed to keep his private and public personas apart. No-one at Homeland Security knew he was gay. If they thought about him at all, they'd probably conclude that he was asexual, just like his computers. That suited Sanderson. Homeland Security was a macho heterosexual place. Coming out of the closet could only lead to trouble. There was still lingering resentment over the President's 'gays in the military' policy.

Most people were dancing. The floor was packed and there was a party atmosphere in the place. As Larry watched, spotlights shone on the three circular tables in the center of the floor, illuminating the table dancers, the stars of the evening. They were all good-looking, well-built young men wearing only the skimpiest of red silk underwear. The choreography was professional, their dancing excellent; always provocative but never lewd. Larry had seen the trio before but he never tired watching them. As he sipped his gin and tonic he couldn't help noticing the fair-haired young man looking at him intently from the other side of the bar. When he caught his eye the young man smiled. Larry looked away again. He wasn't out to pick up or be picked up.

Tonight, the bartender seemed to be auditioning. Between serving his customers he was dancing on the bar and tucking his tips suggestively down his pants. On one of his gyrations around the bar he deposited another gin and tonic in front of Larry and whispered in his ear:

"Sweetheart, this one's on Joseph," pointing to The fair-haired young man on the other side of the bar, who smiled and lifted his glass in a toast to Larry.

It must have been the numerous gin and tonics thought Larry as he fumbled to get the key into the lock on the door of his apartment. Joseph had insisted on helping him home after he had slipped off the stool at the bar in Xanadu and dazed himself when he cracked his head against the brass footrail. Now Joseph gently took the key from him and turned it in the lock. Inside Larry groped for the light switch. Again Joseph helped and as the lights came on he guided Larry over to the couch in the living room and propped him up on it with pillows.

It seemed ages later but Larry imagined he heard the door opening again, imagined he heard voices, and thought he must be dreaming. He was sure he wasn't asleep but he knew he wasn't awake either. He dreamed that hands were lifting him up in the air and carrying him. Funny how the mind can make dreams and imaginings seem so real, he thought.

He wanted to scratch the tickle on his nose but his right hand wouldn't move. He tried his left hand and it wouldn't move either. He felt panic and his struggle, as well as the smelling salts he'd just been administered, awakened him. As his eyes adjusted to the light, he could see that he was lying on his back on the bed and his wrists and ankles were tied to the bedposts. He was naked.

"Wake-up, sweetheart. Are you ready for some fun?"

He knew it was Joseph. His eyes focused on the voice and he could see him standing at the foot of the bed. But there were two of him. He must be seeing double. He closed and opened his eyes but the double image didn't go away. There were two of them.

"This is my best friend, dear Larry. He wants to join in. You don't mind, do you? Two's fun but three's an orgy. Isn't that right, sweetheart?"

Larry's panic increased. He could feel his heart thumping loudly in his chest.

"Joseph, please stop. I'm not into bondage and pain. Don't do this. Let me up," he pleaded.

But that just aroused chuckles in Joseph and his Best Friend who had now emerged from the shadows with a lighted cigarillo between the fingers of his right hand.

"But my Best Friend here is into bondage and pain in a big way. Especially pain. He just loves to give it, don't you, darling?"

Best Friend said nothing. Instead he blew on the end of his cigarillo till it glowed red and then, without any warning, he stuck it into the sole of Sanderson's right foot. Sanderson's body bucked in agony on the bed but the ties held. He started to scream but Joseph stuck a face-cloth in his mouth and gagged him. Best Friend pulled away the cigarillo from Sanderson's foot and his body stopped fighting. Gradually Joseph removed the gag and Larry could smell his own burnt flesh.

"That's just an appetizer, sweetheart. Are you ready for the main course?"

" What do you want from me?" Larry wheezed. His throat hurt from the screams that were never heard.

"I'll tell you what we want, sweetheart. We want you to tell us what you're working on. We want to know what programs you're running for Homeland Security."

Sanderson felt as though the fire from his foot had suddenly hit his brain. They knew. Somebody had found out what he was working on. Or found out enough and had leaked it. Just as quickly he suddenly felt cold as he realized that Joseph and his Best Friend were terrorists. Maybe even the people that MacDara was looking for.

"That's not a secret. I'm working on the next version of our simulator on anti-terrorism. Everybody knows General Shields' special job in the NSC," said Larry in as controlled a voice as he could muster, still trying to talk his way out of this.

"Wrong answer, sweetheart! Best Friend doesn't like wrong answers, do you, darling?"

Knowing what was about to happen didn't help. It only made it worse. Joseph gagged him again and Best Friend stuck the glowing end of his cigarillo into Sanderson's left foot. He seemed to do it twice as long this time and when Joseph removed the gag it looked as though Sanderson was semi-conscious. Joseph stuck the smelling salts under his nose and slapped him on the cheeks till he was satisfied that Sanderson was fully alert again.

Larry Sanderson had never thought of himself as a brave person. But he'd never been tested. Until now. Now he knew he wasn't brave. He didn't want to be tortured any more. He broke down and pleaded to be set free, promised them anything if they'd spare his life. Joseph gave him some water and Larry Sanderson talked.Told them everything that he knew. About the A.I. system, about Shields, about MacDara, about the Circle of Sodom. He couldn't tell them about General Walker or Tony Thackeray because he didn't know that. But he did tell them about the investigation into Colonel McNab and the Millennium Covenant. Joseph knew when he had finished that he had told them everything. He could recognize a broken man.

"Sweetheart, you did good. You should get a prize. Don't you think so, Best Friend? Sweetheart deserves a prize, doesn't he?"

Before Sanderson knew what was happening, Joseph had gagged him again and Best Friend moved towards him from the foot of the bed. He could see the light glinting on the blade and he knew he was going to die. Somehow he didn't fight it. In those split seconds a serene calm descended on him. When his jugular was sliced open he didn't feel it. He only felt the burning in the soles of his feet. And the wetness that gushed from his throat warming his cold naked body.

It was unusual for computer equipment to be delivered directly to General Shields' office. He only used a PC, a printer and a modem and all of those were delivered and installed personally by Larry Sanderson. The box was sitting on the floor beside his secretary's desk when he returned from lunch at two p.m. on Wednesday.

"What's this, Sally?" asked Shields.

"I don't know, Sir. The label says it's an HP Deskjet printer. A UPS delivery man arrived with it half an hour ago. Did you order a new printer?"

"No, I did not. Get me Sanderson on the phone."

"I tried to get him already, Sir. But nobody knows where he is. He didn't show up today."

"That's not like Sanderson. Did you try his home number?"

"Yes, Sir. But he's not there. Only his answering machine. I left a message."

"OK, Sally. Please call Operations and have them send someone up here to check this out. I'll be in my office. Keep trying to contact Sanderson. Let me know when you get him. I want to talk with him."

Half an hour later the intercom buzzer rang on General Shields' phone. It was Sally.

"Still can't find Sanderson. But Ops are here to open your package. Maybe you'd like to see what's in it."

"Thanks, Sally. I believe I will take a look."

As General Shields opened his office door the young man from Operations had just finished opening the box. He looked distressed and was backing away from the box as Sally reached it. Bart Shields was just in time to catch her as she fainted into his arms. He looked down into the box only to be met by the fixed stare from Larry Sanderson's severed head sitting on a bed of ice cubes.

DUBLIN – Dirty Old Town

"Dirty Old Town" is a song, written by **Ewan MacColl,** that was made popular by the Dubliners

The Last Blow

Bob McArdle was Marty Rainey's closest friend, perhaps his only friend. About the same age and similarly saddled with life's infirmities, they met about once a week to bemoan the brave New Ireland. They usually met for lunch, fish and chips for both of them, and then, if the weather was dry, they'd sit near the canal not far from Portobello Road and watch the swans.

Today they sat silently looking at the swans until Marty said, "Bob, will you do something for me?"

Bob looked at him very strangely, "That's a strange question. If I can do it, I'll do it. You know that. Unless it's a bank job. Can't run as fast anymore!" And then chuckled at his own sense of humour.

"I want you to keep something for me."

"Sure, what is it."

Marty pulled a large envelope out of his pocket. He held it in his hand as he looked at Bob.

"There's a tape in here. It's a recording of a phone call. I want you to look after it for me. And, if anything happens to me, I want you to give this to the right person."

"Does this have anything to do with all that tribunal business?"

"It does. But it's even bigger than that. And there are some people who would like to get their hands on what's on the tape. That's if they knew I had it."

"Marty, are you in any kind of trouble?"

"I'll be honest with you, I am. That's why I'm giving you this to keep for me."

"You need protection. Are you talkin' to the gardai?"

"They're the last people I'd be talkin' to. Can't trust anybody."

"But you said I should give this to the right person if anything happens to you. How will I know the right person?"

"That's where I'm relyin' on you. Don't give it to the police or the tribunal or anybody in the government."

"That's everybody!"

"No, you have to find someone you can trust. Somebody who's not afraid to go public with this tape, get it in the papers, on the TV, whatever. Somebody who's not afraid of them."

"I dunno, Marty. I just dunno. You can't let anything happen to you. Do ye hear me, do ye?"

Marty put his big arm around Bob and gave him a hug. Then he slipped the envelope into his hand, got up and walked away.

That was the last time that Bob McArdle would ever see Marty Rainey. Marty was found next day lying face-down on his kitchen floor The door keys were still in his right hand. His throat had been cut. A professional job.

At thirty-four Sean White had buried his father and moved back into the family home to take care of his sixty-five year old mother in the early stages of dimentia.

Married at nineteen, separated at twenty-one, and divorced in 2003 when Ireland finally made divorce legal. Sean had led a hedonist lifestyle for the past ten years. Gifted with boundless energy, his big open face acted as a magnet for many young ladies. But as soon as any relationship turned serious, Sean moved on. He feared commitment, fearing failure itself. But his lifestyle had worn thin in the past three years and had turned into too many hung-over mornings that were beginning to affect his career. A top investigative journalist, he'd been threatened often. He hadn't made the front page in a long time. Only his talent had saved him but he knew that that wouldn't last. So, in a sense, his father's death and the need to care for his mother saved him.

It was eleven on Saturday morning and he was in the kitchen preparing tea and toast for his mother when he heard the phone ring. She answered it and he could tell from her voice and her questions that she felt uncomfortable.

Probably another damn sales call, he thought.

He walked through to the hallway and found his mother standing there with the phone in her hand, looking bewildered, "I don't know who this is. But he says he wants to speak to you, Sean."

Sean took the phone from his mother and said, "Hello."

Spluttering coughs came over the line, followed by, "Is this Sean White?"

"Yes, who's speaking?"

More coughing, then, "I'm a friend of Marty Rainey."

Taken aback, Sean said nothing.

The man sounded elderly and unwell as he continued, "Marty was my closest friend. He gave me something before he died."

Sean asked, "What's your name?"

"Never mind that. I'll tell you when we meet."

"Why are you calling me/"

"I didn't know what to do or who to call. Marty didn't trust anybody. Not even the gardai. He gave me an envelope. Told me, if he died, to give it to the right person. I asked him who. But he said he'd trust me to find the right person."

"And why me?"

"I've seen your name on all the stories about Marty. About the documents too. Marty's documents. I know that. They killed him for them, didn't they?"

"Yes, they did!"

"Well, I want you to have whatever's in this envelope Marty gave me."

"Where do you want to meet?"

"I live near Marty. Harold's Cross. Meet me at *Peggy Kelly's*. Nine tonight."

"OK, I'll be there. And I want to bring somebody with me."

"Who?"

"Dave Smith. He's a trusted colleague. And it pays to be careful, doesn't it?"

The incessant coughing and spluttering had returned, finally followed by a wheezing, "Alright."

Bob McArdle left his house at eight and crossed the canal near the house where the Irish patriot, Robert Emmett, had been arrested. Aided by a strong blackthorn walking stick, he gritted his teeth against the pain of his sciatic nerve as it flowed through his right hip and down his thigh. But, at eighty-three, he'd learned to live with pain. Propelling himself on his blackthorn, he intended to be at *Peggy Kelly's* by nine.

Sean White and Dave Smith walked through the door of *Peggy Kelly's* at exactly eight-thirty. A big, bustling, neighbourhood pub, it was filled with people, young and old, eating, drinking, talking, laughing, enjoying. An infectious atmosphere.

Taking a pint of Guinness and a pint of Carlsberg from the bar, they squeezed their way through and found stools at a small round table in the rear.

"If you don't know who he is, Sean, do you at least know what he looks like?"

"No. But he knows what I look like and he said he'll find me. So we'll have to depend on that."

Dave raised his beer and clinked Sean's Guinness with a "Slainte!"

Taking a long, satisfying sip of his Guinness, Sean looked at Dave and said, "I think this whole Tribunal business is only scratching the surface."

"What do you mean?"

"Come on, they're getting nowhere. You know that. You could fill a library with the testimony they've taken."

"Do you know a better way?"

"There's got to be. It's costing the taxpayer a fortune. And making more fecking millionaires out of the lawyers!"

"Look at the big picture. We have to stop the culture of corruption. End the days of the gombeen man. This is a modern democracy and the old ways have to go. You could view these tribunals as an indictment of the past and a bridge to the future."

"I'll let the historians tell us that when they look back at this time. Maybe you'll be right. But I wouldn't bet on it. We're floating in money. And that's too much temptation."

"I know, I know. But, dammit, we need to send a message to these people! And to the countries and businesses that invest and trade with us. That we are honest and can be trusted. Right now they're waiting to hear from us. And the tribunals are a message to them as well."

"Ok, Ok. But I still say we're spending a ton of money on these tribunals. And for what? Have we arrested anybody? Jailed anybody?"

"No, not yet. Have faith. Look at it from another angle. We've exposed some of these people. Left them with tarnished images. They'll never run for political office again. They'll never hold positions of trust in this country again. Let's face it, they're finished!"

"That's too soft a landing for some of these bastards. They should be in Mountjoy, on bread and water, for the next twenty years!"

"You're right. And if the Tribunal finds enough hard evidence they'll be happy to turn it over to the DPP."

"I wish I could believe that."

"Damn it, you know we're not going to depend on the Tribunal to stop them!"

"I'm sorry. I get so pessimistic at times."

They both realized that they had got so caught up in their conversation that they'd forgotten entirely about the reason they were there.

"It's 9:15 already."

"Shit, I almost forgot."

"No sign of anybody yet."

"No. But he sounded old. And sickly. So I'm not surprised he's late."

Sean took their two empty glasses up to the bartender and said, "*Agus aris!*"

A light drizzle obscured Bob McArdle's glasses. Couples scurried past him and a stray dog almost tripped him. Distracted, he didn't see the two balaclava hooded men step out of a doorway as he hobbled along. One kicked the blackthorn stick out of his hand while the other kicked him in the ribs as he fell. He screamed in pain but the sounds died in his throat as the first assailant wielded the blackthorn like a baseball bat, cracking McArdle's cheekbone and forcing his broken dentures down his throat, blocking his windpipe. Swinging the blackthorn again, he smashed it into McArdle's back before tossing it on the ground. Dying now, his blood merging into the rain and running in rivulets into the drain near his head, the last blow of the blackthorn was unnecessary. The few people who saw the assault fled to the other side of the street. Assuming it to be another gangland killing, they knew it didn't pay to interfere or to even be seen. As the two assailants disappeared, another man, tall and sinister in a long *Jack Murphy* raincoat, stepped out from the shadows and kneeled at Bob McArdle's side. He fished an envelope out of McArdle's pocket. Then he stood and disappeared into the shadows.

At 10:30 Sean White and Dave Smith decided to call it an evening. They speculated that their appointee may have been too ill to show up. They reckoned that, if the caller had been real, they could only hope that he'd call Sean again.

Neither of them connected this with the news item in the next day's paper about the brutal bludgeoning death of a frail old man three streets away from *Peggy Kelly's*.

Who killed Hammarskjold ?

The Gulag

Prisons located in the bleakest localities of eastern Siberia - Kuzbas on the Tom' river.

At the Imperial Hotel in Moscow, Owen MacDara sank into the large antique bathtub to soothe his shattered body. Once in bed he slept until ten a.m. and woke telling himself that four hours sleep was better than none. He shaved, dressed quickly, and then hooked up his laptop and dialed into General Shield's e-mail system. One message waited for him:

Owen:

The President received today the enclosed document from Boris Yeltsin. It's from the KGB archives and shows the involvement of agents of the KGB and CIA in the death of Dag Hammarskjold in the Congo in 1961. We believe there's a connection with the killing of Alexander Ridge.

Find Zhukov if he is still alive and try and get him to talk.

Bart.

The attached image of the KGB document read:

Top Secret
Special Folder

Committee of State Security of the USSR
March 19, 1968 No. 762-Ch
Moscow

TO THE CENTRAL COMMITTEE of the CPSU

Results of the investigation into the death of UN Secretary-General Dag Hammarskjold in the Congo in 1961

Anti-Soviet elements within the Communist Party are engaged in efforts to undermine the Soviet State and enrich themselves. They are in collusion with the Russian mafia and international criminal elements. They are also being used by Capitalist subversives who want to undermine and overthrow the USSR. They are engaged in the distribution of anonymous materials containing terrorist statements against leaders of the CPSU and the Soviet government. A significant number of incidents of anonymous material distribution occurred in Ukraine, Kazakhstan, Latvia, Lithuania, Moscow and Leningrad.

We have uncovered evidence that these same anti-Soviet elements worked to undermine the efforts of the USSR in Africa, most especially in the Congo where they were involved with American capitalist elements to enrich themselves and ensure that their puppet, Mobutu, became the leader of the Congo. We believe that the UN Secretary-General had become aware of this conspiracy and was about to take measures to defeat them. We have strong evidence that criminal agents of the KGB, the CIA and MI5 working in collusion planned the death of Hammarskjold and that mercenaries paid by these people tampered with the Secretary-General's plane.

The KGB is available to provide materials to the Central Committee showing clear evidence of our findings.

For your information
Committee Chairman *   /s/ V. Kherikov*

Strong diagonal lines had been drawn across the document and the order to DESTROY handwritten in bold letters and signed by Georgy Zhukov. "Obviously, someone failed to obey Zhukov's order," MacDara said aloud to himself.

A couple of days search turned up Zhukov. He had been pensioned out of the KGB but it was a search of Moscow's administrative records that did it. Georgy Zhukov had applied to the city in 1992 to take ownership of his Moscow apartment and the records were recent and available.

No one answered at the apartment. MacDara turned to leave as the door to the next apartment opened and a buxom lady emerged. Seeing Owen, she told him that Georgy would not return until September. "He's in Safonikha with his vegetables," she said.

Safonikha is a small village sixty miles northwest of Moscow. MacDara asked an elderly man, the first person he saw, if he knew where Georgy Zhukov lived. "Everybody knows where Zhukov lives," the old man said, and pointed to a house a couple of kilometers away. Zhukov's one-room log house sat in the middle of flat open country, surrounded by some apple trees, and bordered on all sides by orderly green rows of well tended vegetables. He found Georgy Zhukov bent over, hoeing his potatoes. Zhukov was hard of hearing and Owen had to shout his name before he straightened up and looked around. "Georgy Zhukov?"

"Da. What do you want?"

"I want to talk to you. I've come a long way to see you. From Washington."

"Go away. Leave me alone!"

"I can't. You need to help me. I need to know what happened in the Congo. I need to know about Hammarskjold's death."

Georgy Zhukov straightened his spine beyond

the ability of his seventy years, held his hoe like a regal staff and looked long and hard at Owen MacDara. He seemed to be making a judgment, a decision. Owen waited. Finally he asked Owen to follow him and he propped the hoe against the wall before he entered his one-room peasant's home, furnished from strong wood, toughened and scarred from years of use. Owen had brought a gift, a bottle of good single-malt Scotch whisky. He gave it to Zhukov whose face warmed at the sight. He held it up and looked at it. He didn't open it, just reached up and stood it on top of a cupboard. He pointed to a chair, inviting Owen to sit down.

Owen took the chair that was offered and sat down at the table. Georgy Zhukov returned with a plate of sliced cucumber and a large bottle of samogon, homemade vodka, and two glasses. He poured out generous portions and then sat back.

"I could ask you to go away. But there is something in your eyes. Who are you?"

"My name is Owen MacDara. I am working for the President of the United States. Let me tell you what has happened." Owen started with the killing of Alexander Ridge, an event that was news to Georgy Zhukov and ended with a copy of the KGB document that he had received from General Shields. "Now you know why I need to talk with you. Whatever happened in the Congo in '61 is not over. Someone knows. And we think they killed Ridge."

Georgy took a large mouthful of the strong samogon and Owen instinctively followed only to find his throat seared and his face turning firey from the brew. Georgy smiled and gave him time to recover. "I am not a criminal. I was not corrupt. Do you think I would be working like a dog at my age just to stay alive? Just to have some food for the winter. This place has been in my family for generations. But all the old ones are gone. Soon I will be gone too. If I had to live on my KGB pension I would not make it."

Zhukov lifted the glass to his lips and emptied it. It seemed to fill him with a burst of energy and he continued. "The Congo is the heart of Africa. It sits in the middle of that great continent between north and south, east and west. Do you think that *perestroika* and *glasnost* began with Gorbachev? Nyet! That didn't happen overnight. For years many of us wanted change. But we had to work inside the system to do it. So maybe the Soviets were right. We were subversives. Anarchists. But we wanted to stop them from expanding. And we wanted to free our people. Da! Maybe the KGB were right. Maybe we did work with capitalist criminals. But sometimes you have to get in bed with the devil. Sometimes the end justifies the means. Don't you understand?"

"Tell me what happened in the Congo. Did you kill Hammarskjold?"

Zhukov ignored MacDara's question about Hammarskjold and answered in his own fashion. "Do you know what was at stake in the Congo? Uranium! Copper! Minerals! Power! Whoever controlled that controlled Africa. Patrice Lumumba and Moise Tsombe fought over it. Tsombe wanted to control Katanga where all the minerals were. Lumumba wanted Soviet support. The Americans were afraid that Lumumba would win and that the USSR would control the Congo. The heart of Africa would be theirs! Your President – Kennedy – was caught in the middle of all this. He was a liberal, an idealist. He wanted the Africans to shake off their Colonial masters and run their own affairs. But the real power in Washington didn't care about that. They wanted control of Africa's wealth. That's all. So Kennedy became their enemy."

Zhukov stopped, filled the glass in front of him

again, got a second wind and went on. "There were many of us in Russia who wanted our country back too. We are nationalists. The Communist Party are not. So we did not want them to control the Congo. That's why we helped the CIA to kill Lumumba. That's why we got in bed with the devil."

"But why kill Hammarskjold?"

"The UN were up to their eyeballs in the mess. Who do you think captured Tsombe? Da! The UN, that's who!"

"The President needs to know what happened. He needs to know who ordered Hammarskjold's death. He believes whoever killed Ridge wants to know that too. If the world finds out that somebody in Washington ordered the death of Hammarskjold, your Evil Soviet Empire might just be reborn. Do you want to run that risk?"

"Nyet! Nyet! We have come too far to see it all lost." Zhukov picked up the glass he had just filled, put it to his lips, and emptied it in one long gulp. Almost as though it were his last. "I'll tell you. I do not know who were the criminals in Washington. I only know who worked with us. The CIA. His name was Kearns. I never knew his first name."

"And who tampered with the Secretary-General's plane?"

"Ah, yes! I remember him well! A mercenary. Major Lacey. An Irishman, I think. He was businesslike. It was only a job to him. He'd done jobs for us before. Simply for the money. I don't think the Major believed in anything else."

"Where is this Major now?"

"How would I know? I assume he went home after the Congo. That was a long time ago. Is he still alive? We're all getting near the end."

He said that with a sigh, now exhausted after the talk and the painful memories. He finished the last of the bottle, offering none to MacDara, and sat down wearily. He suddenly looked older than his seventy-something years. Owen tried to continue but Georgy Zhukov sat there, staring into the distance, staring at nothing.

MacDara's gut told him that Zhukov wasn't telling him everything but his head told him that he would learn no more. What was Zhukov holding back? And why? Was he protecting someone? Protecting his new Russia? Was he protecting himself? Was he afraid? MacDara looked at the old man again. He just couldn't imagine Zhukov being afraid for himself. Still, old age may have made him more vulnerable. Owen decided that he might never know. At least he had a name: Major Lacey. He'd settle for that. For now.

Zhukov was unkempt, unshaven, dirty and drunk. Vodka spilled out of a half empty bottle clutched tightly in his right fist. He lurched across the road, ranting and raving. Still raving unintelligibly, he waded knee-high into a rain-swollen river. The water swirled around him but he waded even deeper. Now the water was up to his chest and his right arm flourished the vodka bottle over his head. It seemed both a symbol of defiance and a cry for help. His shouting became even louder. Now he was up to his neck in the water and his eyes were bulging out of his head. Suddenly he was out of the river, dripping wet, vodka bottle still in hand, now standing motionless like a statue in the middle of the road. Cars seemed to appear out of nowhere, traveling in both directions, missing him by mere inches. Still he stood there like a rock as though daring them to hit him.

MacDara sensed the rapid noisy beating of his heart; next he sensed fear. Sweat poured off his body and the single sheet that covered him felt damp and clammily cold around his neck. He sat up, turned on the light and reached for his watch: four a.m. He swung his feet onto the floor and into the crumpled pile of his clothes, dropped there when he had fallen drunkenly into bed two hours earlier. He went out to the bathroom and splashed cold water on his face. His heart raced. Alcohol and adrenaline. The deadly combination. Last night he'd really set out to get drunk. Oh yes, he'd known what he was doing. He had wanted it all to go away

This dream, this nightmare, seemed so real. His rational mind told him that the drink caused it. But another deeper sense told him not to be so sure about that. His Celtic sense of life's mysteries insisted that life existed on many levels. Maybe it's an omen. A prophecy. A warning. Some form of ESP brought to life by his night of boozing. Oh yes, he knew he'd pay for it. His body was out of practice. But last night he hadn't given a damn.

It had all started here, at the 'safe house'. The safe house was Dr. Valentin Cretu's – his Moldovan consultant – a man with no particular love for the Russians. Valentin had produced the vodka as soon as he had arrived back from seeing the Insect. Medicine for trauma and shock. But it had soon become obvious as that first bottle emptied that he had wanted more than a painkiller. He had wanted oblivion. He felt his eyes closing again, lay back down and immediately fell into a deep sleep.

Six hours later he woke up with a violent headache. He was slumped upright in an awkward position. The light was still on. He moved and then winced from the pain in his neck muscles. He felt nauseous and stumbled out to the toilet. His attempts at vomiting only succeeded in dry retching. He wished he were dead – out of his misery. Then he swore he'd never do this again. The price was too great. He sat on the floor beside the toilet holding on to the rim of the bowl for support. The cool feel of the ceramic bowl earthed him, brought his mind back in focus. He remembered his dream, his nightmare. He closed his eyes and concentrated. The entire dream came back to him. He saw the drunken Zhukov up to his neck in the river, then standing statue-like in the road as the traffic whizzed past him. The dream was too vivid to dismiss. He determined to see Zhukov. He had to risk it. He needed to see Zhukov anyway. He had always felt that Zhukov had not told him everything. Now he thought he knew what Zhukov was holding back. He needed confirmation of that.

The flight from Moscow to Kemerovo, the regional capital of the Kuzbass region of Russia took a little over four hours. Owen MacDara sat silently beside Dr. Valentin Cretu, staring ahead, blankly, and stupidly. Perfectly in character with his papers which identified him as Dr. Cretu's retarded cousin. To Owen it wasn't too difficult. Unshaven and eyes red rimmed, he still hadn't recovered from his drinking of three nights ago. The morning after that drunken night, Valentin Cretu, at MacDara's insistence, had attempted to find Zhukov. He wasn't at his apartment. He wasn't at his house in Safonikha. No one had seen him lately. A little bribery and couple of cases of vodka soon produced results. It seemed that Zhukov had been arrested for stealing sausages and vodka. He had protested his innocence, but to no avail. He was now in detention, awaiting trial. That could take from eighteen months to two years. There was no bail. Russia's prison system was overcrowded and underfunded. Moscow's overflow is sent to the Kuzbass region in Siberia, the place where the Soviets and the Tsars sent their dissidents, their political foes, and their poets, artists and writers who failed to conform. Many died there from disease, harsh treatment and starvation. Ten thousand people work in the jails of Kuzbass, jails packed with over thirty thousand inmates. Many prisoners spend up to 23 hours a day in their cells. They are undernourished and unhealthy. TB is the biggest scourge of all. Prison hospital colonies are filled with tubercular inmates. That was the destiny of Georgy Zhukov. Dr. Valentin Cretu had learned from his sources, lubricated with sufficient vodka, that Zhukov had TB. He was in Hospital Colony No. 27 in Mariinsk. Dr. Cretu posed as his nephew and requested permission to visit his uncle. Permission was granted. The bureaucracy had become lax and non-existent since the collapse of the Soviet Union.

At Kemerovo a car was waiting for them. A three hour drive through forest and farmland and they were in Mariinsk. Dr. Ivan Malenkov ushered them into his office.

"You may find that your uncle does not know you, Dr. Cretu," said Dr. Malenkov. "He is old and very sick and his mind wanders. Sometimes he doesn't know who he is or where he is."

"I don't understand," said Dr. Cretu. "Six months ago, he was strong and healthy. What happened?"

"Oh, in a way, he did it to himself. He wouldn't eat when he came to Kemerovo. Claimed he was innocent. They all do, you know. Claimed it was a conspiracy. To silence him. Another familiar claim," said Dr. Malenkov, eyeing Owen with some interest, as Owen stared blankly into space, fidgeting with the buttons on his coat, "but, of course, those days are gone. We don't have any political prisoners any more."

"When was he sent here?" asked Valentin.

"About a month ago. When he wouldn't eat he just got weaker. Then he caught TB. We're treating him now. But he needs to take all of his drugs. Every day. Even then it may take up to a year to cure him. But only if he eats and only if he takes all his drugs. He's eating a bit, but not enough. We can't be sure if he's taking all of his drugs. There's been very little improvement in him since he came here. As I said, you're welcome to see him. But he may not know you," said Dr. Malenkov and then, pointing to Owen, said, "What about him?"

"My cousin. He was born like that. Can't speak or hear. But Uncle Georgy loves him. I brought him with me. Just a chance it might help," said Dr. Cretu.

The meeting was over. Dr. Malenkov called in a nurse, a stocky middle-aged, battle-weary woman.

"Nina," said Dr. Malenkov, "take Dr. Cretu and his cousin to see Georgy Zhukov," and then ushered them all out of his office.

Before they saw Zhukov, Nurse Nina asked them to put on white gauze masks to protect themselves.

"It's safer if you wear these. It's better here now than it used to be. But you should still protect yourself. A couple of years ago a third of our patients were dying from TB. We buried about one hundred a month. But now the World Health Organization is helping us. We're getting more money and more drugs," she said.

She turned on her heel and plodded ahead of them to the corner of a ward unit where a hollow-cheeked, frail old man sat on the sagging mattress on his metal-framed bed. He was leaning on a walking stick that anchored him to the floor between his two bony knees. The man who sat there was only a shadow of the strong oak-like Zhukov that Owen had found tilling his vegetables in Safonikha.

Nurse Nina said, "Don't stay with him too long. I doubt if he'll know you, anyway. I'm sorry." She then departed and left them there.

There were no other patients in the ward. Georgy Zhukov looked at them. There was no recognition. Of course, there wouldn't be in the case of Dr. Valentin Cretu. They had never met each other before. And the masks didn't help either, Owen decided. The old man was coughing now, a deep racking cough that shook his frail body. Owen stepped out of range of the cough and pulled down his mask.

"Mr. Zhukov. My name is Owen MacDara. Do you remember me? I went to see you in Safonikha. We talked about the KGB...about the Congo. I told you that the President of the United States had sent me to see you. I asked you about the death of Dag Hammarskjold in the Congo. The U.N. Secretary-General. Do you remember?" asked Owen, watching Zhukov for a sign of recognition, any sign. But Zhukov said nothing, trying to suppress his coughing, and looking intently at Owen. His eyes were bright, abnormally bright, the eyes of one whose mind seemed to be fired by the wasting of his body.

Dr. Valentin Cretu spoke through his mask. "Owen, I'm afraid Dr. Malenkov is right. He doesn't remember you. I doubt that he would know his own mother. I'm afraid you'll learn no more here. Whatever you were looking for is going to stay that way. Maybe that's why Zhukov is here. To shut him up. If it is, they've succeeded."

"Oh, I know that's why he's here. This proud old man would never steal. He was framed. I'm afraid there's nothing we can do for him. Except hope that the drugs ease his pain. OK, let's go," said Owen, putting on his mask again and looking at Zhukov for the last time.

But Zhukov had taken his hands from the walking stick and propped it against the bed. He was unbuckling his belt and pulling it through the loops. Owen stopped and watched. Zhukov slid a long chisel-like thumbnail along a section of the belt and the seam came apart. He reached in with his bony fingers and took something out, something that looked like a piece of paper that had been folded and folded until it wasn't much larger than two postage stamps. He reached out and gave it to Owen. He still didn't speak but there was just the faint trace of a smile at the edge of his lips.

In the car on the return journey to Kemerovo, Owen MacDara gingerly unfolded the piece of paper given to him by Georgy Zhukov. The writing was small, neat, and precise – and Russian. He knew enough of the language to get the gist of it.

Confirmation that the orders to kill Hammarskjold had come from Washington and Moscow.

This was news that would topple the fragile Russian Government.

Key West ...the Conch Republic

"a lawless place where assassinations and other activities are perfectly legal"

Joe Haldeman's *Buying Time*

The Contract

Jimmy Coyne checked into the Reach Hotel, set the combination alarm clock coffee machine for ten a.m. and awakened to the sound of the coffee beans in the grinder. Filling a large mug he opened the sliding glass doors and went out on the patio, feeling the cooling breezes coming in from the blue-green Atlantic. His room, with its cool Mexican tiled floor and warm Indian dhurrie rugs would be hard to leave this morning. But he had a contract to fill which he would, reluctantly.

Harry Evans lived on the east side of Key West, close to Simonton and Duval Streets and only a stone's throw away from The Reach Hotel. Jimmy had no difficulty finding him. He lived in a distinctive two story Conch house, constructed by ship's carpenters in the late nineteenth century. It was adorned by an ornamental balcony that fronted the entire house.

He found Harry Evans sitting in a wicker chair on the porch immersed in the daily papers. He had the virility of a man at least twenty years younger. Coyne introduced himself and Harry seemed resigned. He knew this day would come. He left to bring back some refreshments. When he returned he found Jimmy glancing through a copy of Hemingway's *The Old Man and the Sea* that he'd extracted from a shelf where books were intermingled with works by Hemingway, Turgenev, Joyce and Tom Clancy.

"You know, Jimmy. I think Hemingway had it right after all."

"What do you mean?

"When he killed himself. He knew that life

was only worthwhile if he could still write. He couldn't write anymore."

"But what about his family? Didn't he also have a responsibility to them?"

"He did. But what have you got to offer them if your own life has lost its dignity?"

"This doesn't sound like you at all."

"Oh, I've been lucky, Jimmy. I'm as fit as a fiddle and the old mind still works. I wonder sometimes what I'd have done if it had all started to fail, the body, the mind, the whole shebang. Don't dismiss Hemingway's option as the act of a crazy and selfish person."

"You'll never go like Hemingway."

"I don't have time to think about it. I'm too busy."

Harry Evans walked over to a wall of his study that was covered with photographs, degrees, awards and memberships and took down a group photograph in an antique pine frame. The bullets that penetrated his back shattered the glass on the photograph and left the antique pine frame in splinters.

Back at the Reach, Jimmy Coyne poured himself a Scotch and tried to deal with the contract he'd filled, most reluctantly. He drove back up the Keys by mid-afternoon. The sun was shining and the sky was a deep blue.

A window out of The Conch Republic, he thought, *a lawless place where assassination and other activities are perfectly legal.*

And one play

The Altar Boys

Settings/Ambience

- Pub: **St. Anne's**; small bar with four stools;small round table with two chairs
- A play in two acts
- Background music: Gregorian chants; Glenstall Abbey

Cast

Harry Coyne, a former altar boy, who stayed in Ireland.

Danny Wilson, a former altar boy, who emigrated to the US

Peggy, a local pub owner (*who was never an altar boy*) but who once dreamed of a career on the stage

Act I

The curtain rises on a dimly lit pub, St. Anne's, where one customer, ***Harry Coyne****, is seated at the end of a 4 stool bar.* ***Peggy*** *is tidying up behind the bar.*

Glenstall Abbey's music is playing low in the background – ***Peggy*** *refills* ***Harry's*** *pint.. The pub door swings open and* **a man** *enters. Wearing a long raincoat and a black woollen cap, he takes off the raincoat (dripping wet) and looks for a place to hang it up.* ***Peggy*** *rushes over to help.*

Man: Hellofa night out there!

Peggy: Ach, sure we had no summer at all. Stand over by the fire and warm yourself.

Man: Nothing like a good turf fire.

Peggy *returns behind the bar and the man stands with his back to the fire, then turns around and warms his hands. He walks up to the bar and stands at the opposite end from Harry. He looks over and* ***Harry*** *nods to him. He nods back. No words are exchanged.*

Peggy: What'll you have?

Man: A pint of Guinness.

Peggy *pours the pint and lowers the sound of the music. The man raises the pint half-way to his lips. He is looking across at* ***Harry*** *and suddenly stops and* *walks past the 2 empty stools until he is face to face with* ***Harry.***

Man: Jaysus, Harry, it's not you, is it?

Harry: It's me alright but .....?

The man just stands there with a smile on his face. He moves even closer to ***Harry** ...*

Harry: Danny Wilson! Oh, my God!

Danny: Been a long time, Harry!

They put down their pints and grab each other in a rib crunching hug.

Harry: It's the American accent that threw me off, Danny. I thought you were a yank!

They both burst out laughing at that.

Danny: Been in the States a long time. Twenty years now. Over there they think I'm an Irishman and over here they think I'm an American.

Harry: You haven't changed a bit!
Danny: Hah! Don't bullshit me, Harry! It's great to see you again. It's that music. Thought I was in the chapel. Serving mass. Remember when we were altar boys? Your face jumped into my head. And there you were, sitting there. You didn't have that fuzz on your face the last time I saw you but I'd remember you anywhere!

He looks across at Peggy and says: We're gonna move. We're not running away or anything. I haven't seen this man in years!

Peggy: Take that table. I'll bring over your drinks.

They sit down at the little round table and Harry calls back to Peggy:

Harry: Can you play something else. I can't stand sorrowful Irish music.

Danny: Yeah, that sorrowful stuff kills me too. I'd rather listen to U2.

Peggy yells back:

Peggy: OK! , I'm with Danny. U2 comin' up.

She puts on U2 singing 'Where the streets have no name' but turns it low so it would not interfere with their conversation. She then brings their pints over to the table.

Peggy: What brings you back to Ireland, Danny?

Danny: *The Gathering.* The Consul-General in Miami twisted my arm.

Harry: Jasus, Danny, that's a con job. Did you hear what Gabriel Byrne says about it. Says it's a scheme to rip off the diaspora!

Danny: Yeah, I read that. But, hey, I'm not taking sides. I'll spend a few dollars and maybe that'll help things. But I'll do something better. I'll see old friends like you, Harry. Isn't that the real meaning of *The Gathering.*

Peggy: Sorry I asked, fellas.

And with that, Peggy heads back to the bar.

Danny: Do you remember McKenna?

Harry: The Yank! A bully. He was a bully!

Danny: Jaysus, yeah! He'd been in the States for years. Even had a better American accent than meself. Big, he must have been 6'3" And built like a wrestler. When he moved around that sacristy, real fast just like a Yank, we all trembled.

Harry: Didn't he hit you?

Danny: I'll never forget that. I stumbled and dropped one of the cruets at the door of the sacristy after serving mass. It probably held drops of the blood of Christ. Smashed all over the floor. He went berserk. Grabbed me by the surplus and slapped me on the side of the head. I was terrified.

Harry: I'm surprised that we've survived all that !

Danny: Have we? Have we really?

Suddenly the lights go out in the pub. Peggy finds matches and lights two large candles, leaves one on the bar and carries the other and places it on the centre of Joe and Harry's table.

Peggy: Happens all the time. When we have a storm like this. Sometimes we get it back in an hour. Sometimes it takes a day or two.

*Peggy returns to the bar. They sit in silence for a while, haunting shadows everywhere, the candles flickering, the pints raised to lips and slowly sipped. Finally **Harry** speaks:*

Harry: Thought that was a sign from God. Can you believe it? I'm still full of that old superstition.

Danny: They did a job on our heads! We have not survived. Why do you think I'm an atheist today?

Harry: I don't believe very much of it any more meself ...

Danny: And the whole confession thing scared me too. I got claustrophobia in those confession boxes. I remember being taken to confession at the parish house. No box. Just kneeling on a chair beside the priest.

Harry: At least you could hide in the box. Disguise your voice maybe,

Danny: They bloodywell knew who you were. But sitting out there in the open beside the man. That's really intimidating!

Harry: Who was it?

Danny: Who do you think? Just my luck. It was McKenna! I almost choked when I said '*Bless me father, for I have sinned.*'

Harry: Go on, go on, you can confess to me!

Danny: Making a joke of it, hah!

Harry: Come on, Danny, ease up. It must be funny looking back on it now.

Danny: Well, it wasn't funny on the day. I hated confession. Always made up silly stuff like *'I lied'* or '*I disobeyed my mother'* and kept the hard stuff till the end.

Harry: The hard stuff?

Danny: Oh, hell, you know. I'd say *' I had impure thoughts, Father'* And he'd say ' *Did you act on these impure thoughts, my son'* and I'd say '*No,Father'*. I lied right there in the confessional. I think he was disappointed. Do you think he got it off listening to kids telling him about wanking off? Do you think?

Harry: Shit, that's a good bet! With all the dirt we're digging up about them these days, I wouldn't be surprised.

They sit in silence for a while. The only sounds are the bottoms of their glasses on the table and Peggy gently humming to the music ...finally Danny breaks the silence:

Danny: What's the most bizarre thing you did as an altar boy?

Harry: Bizarre?

Danny: Yeah, I mean odd, weird, something like that.

Harry: I dunno...I was stressed out all the time. Ok – what did you think was the most bizarre thing you did.

Danny: Easy. It was holding the paten under people's tongues when they came up to the altar to receive communion.

Harry: I was always uncomfortable doing that too. But what was bizarre about it?

Danny: People didn't have a choice of taking it on the palm of their hands in those days. They had to stick out their tongue and the priest placed the communion on there while I held the paten under their chins. To pick up any crumbs I suppose.

Harry: Yeah, totally unsanitary, I always thought.

Danny: But it was the tongues. Young and vibrant. Old and wrinkled. Clean and pink. Yellow-glazed. Mottled and dangerous looking. Sometimes bad breath too.

Harry: Oh my God, I remember that. Always thought that I was invading their privacy. Seeing them naked in some way. Especially if I knew the person.

Danny: Absolutely! And when I'd meet them on the street I could only see their tongue. Bizarre!

Harry: Ough, that makes me sick. I need another pint to wash it all away. Maybe we better talk about something else.

Danny: Talk about something else! Are you censoring me?

But **Harry** is already half-way to the bar and **Danny** is yelling this out to the audience. Then he gets up and follows **Harry** to the bar.

Peggy *refills their pints and shows* ***Danny*** *the way to the toilet. He leaves.*

A jig plays in the background. ***Harry*** *grabs* ***Peggy*** *and takes her out from behind the bar. They laugh loudly and deeply and start dancing to the jig.*

In the midst of this, ***Danny*** *returns from the toilet.*

Danny: OK, **Harry,** you wait till I leave the bar! It's my turn.

And he takes ***Peggy*** *away from* ***Harry*** *and starts dancing – a very poor version of a jig.* ***Harry*** *continues to jig alongside them.*

Then the music ends ....

Danny: Been away too long. Lost my touch.

Peggy: Ah, but you altar boys are so romantic!

Harry: Did you hear that, **Danny**. We're romantic!

Danny: **Peggy, Peggy, Peggy,** what are you talking about?

Peggy: I've known a lot of altar boys in my day and I've never met one that wasn't romantic.

Danny (*laughing out loudly*): We learned it all on the *Altar of Romance*, ye know, the learning stage of *The Ballroom of Romance*!

*They all start laughing uncontrollably, then **Danny** and **Harry** take their pints and return to the table.*

Danny: I lived in fear of Sunday mornings

Harry: But we never told anybody

Danny: Tell anybody! Who would have listened to us? And, hell, we weren't wimps.

***Harry** gets up and dances around the table, singing 'we weren't wimps', 'we weren't wimps' until **Danny** asks him to quit. **Harry** sits down again.*

Danny: Dammit, **Harry,** this isn't a comedy show!

Harry: It could be. Think about it. There's great material in this altar boy stuff. It could be a hit. *The West End! Broadway! Hollywood!* You're a writer. You can do it.

Danny: That's crazy! Even if I could, can you imagine what would happen to me. I'd be driven out of the country. Just like O'Casey.

Harry: Agh, you're being melodramatic. Ireland isn't like that anymore.

Danny: You think? I wouldn't be so sure.

Harry: The country's changed. They're ready to hear from the hidden voices of the altar boys. Sure *Fifty Shades of Grey* is in every bookstore in the country.

*They sip their pints in silence for a minute until **Harry** breaks the silence.*

Harry: So, tell me anyway, what made you afraid?

Danny: Everything! Sitting on the altar facing the congregation as McKenna preached 'fire and damnation' and talked about beating the hedgerows at night for courting couples.

Harry: He did that?

Danny: Yip! With a big blackthorn stick!

Harry: Jaysus!

Danny: And I'd sit on that altar, red faced, thinking that the congregation would believe I was guilty of every sin he screamed about!

Harry: That would scare me alright!

Danny: Well, it did. I was scared every Sunday.

Danny: Some of the things we did was sacrilegious ... but what did we know?

Harry: That's right, what did we know.

Danny: Remember, we used to parody some of the Latin stuff.

Harry: *Tantum ergo, make Sam's hair grow …*

Danny: *Ora pro nobis, Oh rap your nose up …*

And they both stand up and sing in unison:

Harry: *Tantum Ergo*
Danny: *Make Sam's hair grow*
Harry: *Ora pro nobis*
Danny: *Oh, rap your nose up*

'Agus aris' *yells* ***Peggy*** *from the bar – and they do it again (hopefully to the applause of the audience) – she has come out from behind the bar and is clapping loudly.*

It's nearing the end – closing time. They are both tipsy now, too many pints, too many emotional memories. **Harry** and **Danny** stagger away from the table and start to waltz each other across the floor. **Peggy** is tidying up the bar, gathering glasses…she has six shot glasses sitting on a tray.

Danny *sees them, staggers over to the bar, picks them up and yells:*

'Look out for the cruets. Watch them tumble. Isn't it cruel to tumble the cruets'

Peggy: **Danny,** stop it! You'll break them!

Harry: Aw, **Danny**, forget the fecking cruets. Let's dance!

Danny *puts the shot glasses back on the bar and asks, in slurred tones,*
What will we dance about?

Harry: The Gathering.

Danny: The Gathering. What gathering?

Harry: The Gathering of the Altar Boys

Danny: An altar boys Gathering! Are you crazy?

Peggy: That's a brilliant idea, **Harry**!

Danny: Yeah, **Peggy**, you can round up all those romantic altar boys. It'll be one hell of a gathering ...

Act II

We must wait for The Gathering

Pat Mullan

Pat Mullan is a thriller writer, poet, and artist. He was born in Ireland and has lived in England, Canada and the USA. He now lives in Connemara, in the west of Ireland.

You can visit him at: www.patmullan.com

www.ingramcontent.com/pod-product-compliance
Lightning Source LLC
Chambersburg PA
CBHW052007240626
47153CB00008B/2780
9780983865261